Best Friends

~~FOOTBALL~~

PLAYBOOK

A.W. Downer

CHICKEN SCRATCH BOOKS

www.chickenscratchbooks.com

Chicken Scratch Books
PO Box 104
Wisdom, MT 59761
www.chickenscratchbooks.com

Publisher's Note: This is a work of fiction. Names, characters, places, and incidents are a product of the author's imagination. Locales and public names are sometimes used for atmospheric purposes. Any resemblance to actual people, living or dead, or to businesses, companies, events, institutions, or locales is completely coincidental.

Ordering Information: Special discounts are available on quantity purchases by corporations, associations, and others. For details, contact the publisher at the address above.

First Chicken Scratch Books Printing, 2021

ISBN 978-1-953743-08-4 (paperback)
ISBN 978-1-953743-09-1 (ebook)

Printed in the United States of America

Dedicated to my childhood friends whose
lifelong friendships inspired this story.

CHAPTER 1

Hannah raced down the field, her cleats kicking up clods of turf. The crowd screamed with anticipation. If she could make a touchdown in these last few seconds, they'd win the game. The NFL would be sure to draft them. Hannah dashed between two blockers, ducking to avoid their outstretched arms. She was free at the twenty yard line.

"I'm open! I'm open!" She turned to watch for the ball, to see it soaring through the air, to catch it safely in the cradle of her arms, but there was no ball. The quarterback stood frozen in time, arm raised but unmoving.

"Throw it! Throw it! I'm open!" Hannah jumped and waved her arms, trying to get the QB's attention.

The QB finally turned. Instead of throwing the ball, she stared blankly at Hannah. "I have to go to school."

Wham! Three of the other team's linebackers tackled Hannah to the ground, knocking all the air out of her.

Whoa.

Time out!

The stadium vanished. In a moment, the shouts of the crowds, the smell of hot dogs and pizza, the feel of her uniform and helmet—all disappeared. Hannah stood in her own backyard again. The August air was sticky-hot, and sweat dripped down the back of her neck.

Beth stood in front of her, her eyes glazed, the football cupped loosely in her hand. Her face was red from playing in the afternoon sun, and her wavy hair had frizzed all over the place.

"What did you say?" Hannah had been so into the game she must have heard wrong. Beth had been acting kind of weird all afternoon, but still, she must have heard wrong.

"I have to go to school," Beth repeated.

All the air squished out of her lungs, as though she were still on the bottom of a pile. Both teams were on her now, and the football was under her, pushing into her rib cage.

"What do you mean, 'go to school'?" It was a little late for summer school. Craft school or some dumb extracurricular like that? Or . . . or . . .

"My parents are putting me into private school."

Beth dropped the ball. It rolled away and bounced off the patio.

No way. No way, no way!

Hannah jumped over to Beth, pounding her feet into the ground each time she landed.

"No! No. This . . . can't . . . be . . . happening." She grabbed Beth by the shoulders and shook her. "Tell me this isn't happening!"

Beth pushed her away and stepped back. She swallowed hard. That wasn't Beth. Beth didn't push her away. She was never serious. Beth wasn't serious.

No, she was serious. She meant it.

She was going to school.

"They can't put you in school!"

"Well, they are."

"But why?" The sun seemed to grow hotter, making it harder to breathe.

"The baby." Beth sank cross-legged to the ground. "Mom said she has to spend so much time with the baby that she can't focus on my school anymore."

But . . . but . . . Hannah turned and stomped several paces away. "But we're going into middle school. We're in sixth grade now. We can do school on our own."

"I tried that one. Mom said middle school is more complicated, so we will need help."

That was so not true. Hannah stomped back the

other way, waving her arms.

The game isn't over; just try another play.

"Well, then—what if my mom taught you? We're in the same grade. We already do science together on Wednesdays."

Beth sighed so hard she looked like she might break apart.

"I tried that one, too. Mom said your mom has enough on her hands with you, Zach, and Olivia."

So, this was *their* fault. Little siblings ruin everything.

"We'll do the 'public school is bad for your kid' campaign. I've still got all the articles. We'll just cross out public and write in private."

Beth half-smiled. "Mom knows that one. Besides, it didn't work for anyone else."

No. All their other friends had gone to school, too, despite all the articles. Hannah and Beth were the only ones left.

Until now.

The entire team had been traded.

Hannah dropped onto the ground and stared across at Beth. All the summer energy leaked out, leaving her like the empty stadium after a game.

"So, you're really going to school?"

Beth nodded. Her eyes sparkled, and then tears were flowing down her cheeks. "And I have to wear a uniform! It's a plaid *skirt*. I'm gonna die, Hannah!"

Hannah bit her lip and blinked rapidly.

Eleven-year-olds don't cry. Middle schoolers don't cry.

She lay back and blinked up at the sky. The sweet smell of grass drifted over her. This wasn't fair. Not Beth. She'd handled all their other friends going to school because Beth had always been here, would always be here.

A cloud rolled by shaped like the Green Bay Packers *G*. Their team: hers and Beth's. Hannah watched until it disappeared over the roof. Who would she throw passes with at park day? Who would she do science with? Who would she pick co-op classes with?

This couldn't be happening.

The screen door squeaked open, and Mom stuck her head out.

"Beth! Your mom is here!"

Hannah didn't want to ask, but she had to know. "When do you start?"

"The last week of August."

Figured.

A week earlier than normal. That was just one of the many reasons going to school was the worst.

Beth appeared in Hannah's vision, looking down at her. "I'll see you later?"

"Yeah. See ya later."

It had finally happened. Hannah Taylor and Beth Singleton had been picked up for the best team in the whole NFL: the Green Bay Packers. But instead of being second string, Beth was going straight to starting quarterback while Hannah had been put on the practice squad.

Hannah sank onto the bench and stared out at the empty stadium. Empty seats, empty boxes. The fans had gone home. The team was in the locker room. The stadium was completely silent, except for one pesky bird.

Beth sat down beside her. "It's okay. We'll get you on the active roster soon."

"Yeah, if someone gets hurt." Hannah kicked her cleats against the turf.

"Maybe I should throw the ball in someone's face. You know, on accident." Beth winked.

Hannah chuckled. They might not be able to play together, but at least they were technically on the same team.

The screen door creaked again, and Mom came into Hannah's vision. Hannah rolled over, resting her chin on her hands. She did not feel like talking. Mom knelt beside her.

"Are you okay?" Mom patted her back.

She didn't move.

"Mrs. Singleton told me they're putting Beth in private school."

Hannah blinked. Maybe Mom could convince the

Singletons not to do it. She leaned up on her elbows and gazed into Mom's face.

"Did you tell her what a bad idea that is? That Beth won't adjust so she'll get bad grades and how the teachers don't care about the students or about the hours and hours of homework Beth will have to do?"

Mom smiled, but it was her 'oh honey' smile, not a 'yes, and Mrs. Singleton agreed with me' smile.

"Teachers do care about their students, Hannah. But that's beside the point. It's not my place to tell the Singletons what to do. They have to do what they can to give Beth the best education. If Mrs. Singleton can't focus on Beth's schooling, then maybe private school is the best choice."

"What about *my* education?" Hannah sat up and put her hands on Mom's knees. "How am I supposed to get a good education when there's no one to hang out with? I'll be a social outcast, like people always think homeschoolers are!"

"Not everyone thinks that, Hannah." Mom smiled again. This wasn't funny. "You'll get plenty of social-ization at park days and co-op."

"Socializing with *who*? All my friends have gone to school. The world's parents are against me!" Hannah flopped over and buried her face in her arms.

Mom patted her leg. "Maybe you'll make new friends this year."

Hannah stared up at Mom. "With *who*?" Mom was not getting the point. "There isn't even anyone my age anymore, much less someone to play sports with. It was hard enough throwing passes with just me and Beth."

"You made it work."

Hannah cocked her eyebrows at Mom.

"Maybe someone new will have joined this year."

"The only people who ever join the homeschool group have little kids."

"That's not true." Mom stroked Hannah's back like she used to do when Hannah was Olivia's age. "Do you remember when Cassie moved away?"

Of course Hannah remembered. She and Cassie had been best friends forever, ever since she could remember. She hadn't needed other friends because she'd had Cassie. They'd started soccer together when they were five.

"You were devastated," Mom said. "You didn't think you'd ever be happy again. But when we got to the first park day of the year, there was a new family with a little girl just your age and just as excited about sports."

"Beth."

"So, maybe that will happen again this year."

Maybe.

Hannah couldn't imagine finding *another* Cassie

or Beth. But there had been other friends who liked to play sports and throw passes. Maybe there would be this year, too.

Hannah closed her eyes. That pesky bird was still chirping.

What would she ever do without Beth?

CHAPTER 2

Hannah lay on Beth's bed wearing her green and yellow swimsuit for the end-of-summer pool party. She traced the outline of one of the helmets on Beth's official NFL Green Bay comforter, soft and worn. The green had faded. Mom and Dad wouldn't let Hannah get one. They said her room was too Packery already, and besides, they were expensive.

Beth's room was where they always got ready for the end-of-summer pool party and half their soccer matches. The trophies they had won together sat proudly on her green dresser (with yellow drawer pulls). Between the bed and the dresser was a fluffy green rug with the Green Bay *G* on it. The curtains, which were closed so she could change, were a pale yellow with green *G*'s covering them. Her room was like an advertisement for NFL merchandise.

Beth stood in front of her full-length Green Bay mirror, staring at her reflection. Her new school uniform was definitely not official NFL. It wasn't even green and yellow. The 'blouse', as Mrs. Singleton called it, was a button-down white shirt with a patch that looked like a medieval shield on the left pocket. The skirt was puke-red plaid with tiny yellow stripes and huge pleats. Not cool. Literally. It was made of flannel or wool or something, scratchy and hot.

If Hannah's parents ever tried to force her into a uniform, it would be like a game between the worst team in the NFL and the Super Bowl champs for five years running. She wouldn't be caught dead in a skirt.

Beth turned a circle, then picked up an edge of the skirt and dropped it. She curled her lip.

"What even is a skirt's purpose? If we have to wear uniforms, why couldn't they have picked jerseys? They're so much more functional."

Hannah shrugged. "It's school. They're paid to torture you."

Beth flopped onto the bed. "This is so unfair. Every afternoon, all I'm going to think about is how you're probably done with school already and how I could have you over if I weren't stuck in school being tortured out of my mind."

Hannah put her chin on her hands and stared in

front of her. She could just see their reflections in the mirror. Beth's uniform was pretty awful.

"Yeah, well, I might be done with school, but I'll be bored to death, too. I can't have anyone over either—you're all still in school." She sighed. "We'll never get to see each other."

Ouch.

It sounded even worse when she said it out loud. Beth's reflection looked down in defeat.

But it wasn't really that bad. Hannah still saw their other friends—the ones who had gone to school—just not as often.

Suddenly, Beth bounced up onto her knees. "What about the games? We can still see each other almost every week if we watch the Packers games together."

Hannah sat straight up and turned to her friend. She was right. "We still have to spend the night sometimes, too."

"Then we'll see each other twice a week. It's not the end of the world." Beth's eyes were glistening, silently pleading for Hannah to agree that it wasn't the end of the world.

Hannah grinned and lightly punched her shoulder. "You're right. It won't be that bad as long as we watch the games together."

At least the Packers games weren't during school hours. Not having Beth at park days or co-op was bad enough, but if she missed the games, that really would be the end of the world.

Mom said there would be someone new in the homeschool group this year, someone Hannah could throw passes with while Beth was at school. There had to be. But if there was an awesome new friend this year, and even if that friend was a Packers fan, Beth would still be Hannah's best best friend. And they'd always watch games together.

Mrs. Singleton called up the stairs, "Are you girls ready?"

"Almost!" Beth shouted. She ran into the closet and came out a minute later in her own green and yellow swimsuit. Packers green and yellow.

Best best friends green and yellow.

CHAPTER 3

The smell of chlorine bit Hannah's nose as they entered the pool enclosure. The end-of-summer swim party was the first official event of the new school year, which meant any new members of the homeschool group might be there, though they often didn't show up until the first park day.

The party had already started, judging by the sounds of splashing and screaming. Hannah surveyed the group crowded on the deck chairs and playing in the water. Little kids, little kids, moms, high schoolers.

No middle schoolers. No one new.

Well, at least for today, Beth was with her.

They found Hannah's mom rubbing sunscreen onto Olivia at a group of deck chairs. Mom looked up.

"Hi, Hannah! Did you girls have fun?"

"Yup." Hannah laid her towel on the deck chair next to Mom's bag.

"Oh, Hannah," Mom said. "Will you help Olivia with her life vest while I sunscreen Zach?"

Hannah stopped herself from rolling her eyes just in time. "Mom."

"Hannah."

Hannah sighed. *The oldest always has to do everything.*

She went to where Olivia stood in her pastel pony swimsuit. Hannah couldn't think of a single football team with hot pink or soft purple in their team colors. Although, there might be one with turquoise.

She picked up Olivia's pink life vest. "Hold still, squirt."

Olivia beamed up at Hannah with her large, dark eyes. "Are you gonna swim with me?"

Not unless Mom made her. Olivia couldn't actually swim, and Hannah would be stuck in the shallow end if that happened. "No. I'm going to swim with Beth."

Olivia held up her stuffed rabbit, which was desperately in need of a wash. "Want to give Fluffy a kiss?"

"No. Now hold still." Hannah clicked the buckle and patted Olivia's back. "There you go, squirt. Have fun." She turned to where Beth stood waiting.

"Are you ready?" Beth asked, but she didn't sound annoyed. She understood having to do things for siblings.

Hannah bounced on her toes. "Let's do jumps off the deep end."

"I know what we should do first!" Beth jumped into the air. "The Lambeau Leap!"

They took off running over the textured concrete.

"Walk!" several moms yelled.

And she'd done it! She scored the winning touchdown in a seventy-yard dash—the most amazing *touchdown in Green Bay history! Hannah did a victory dance in the end zone and spiked the football. Now came her favorite part! She ran toward the crowd and leaped into the stands.*

Splash! Cold water crashed over her head. She pushed off the bottom of the pool and swam back to the surface. Jumping into the stands for real had to be painful. People are lumpier than water. Hannah turned toward the deep end. Beth jumped into the stands and landed right next to her, splashing her with a tidal wave.

Nice one!

Hannah swam to the edge of the pool and pulled herself out.

A group of girls, probably a year or two younger, had taken over the deep end. Each one held her arms over her head in a circle and twirled around on tiptoes before jumping in. They looked like those clips of football players learning ballet to help with their coordination and balance and stuff. Those girls didn't look as though they wanted to play sports, though. They looked like they just wanted to do ballet.

Ick.

"What should we do this time?" Hannah asked as the last ballet girl jumped in.

"How about a field kicker who slips on the wet grass?"

Hannah laughed.

Perfect.

The slipping field kicker jump hurt. Hannah hadn't thought about how they would land on their backs.

Next, they did tackling and being tackled.

Hannah popped out of the water after a trying-to-catch-an-interception jump. Beth surfaced right beside her.

"Are you hungry?" Hannah asked.

"Oh, yeah."

Climbing out of the pool, they grabbed their towels and went to the snack tables to see what there was.

"Look at these!" Beth held up some pretzels shaped like footballs and helmets. Hannah popped one into her mouth and sucked off the salt.

17

"Hi, girls." Mrs. Singleton appeared at Beth's side. "It looked like you were having fun out there."

Hannah squinted her eyes at her. Cool moms don't send their kids to school.

Bad call. Bad call.

"Okay, Beth, it's time to get ready to go."

But it wasn't even the fourth quarter! This was one bad ref.

"Now? It's not even dark yet," said Beth.

"You want to be sure you get enough rest the night before your first day of school. Meet me at the car in five minutes."

Hannah glared as Mrs. Singleton walked away.

Beth put down the bag of pretzels and hugged her arms. "I guess I should go."

She turned and walked away, like a retiring quarterback leaving the field for the last time, except no one in the crowd was cheering. They were just sad.

What an awful end to a game.

The games!

"Oh!" Hannah pulled her towel tight and chased Beth to the parking lot, ignoring the way the asphalt bit into her feet. "You are coming over in two weeks, right?"

Beth spun around. "For the game? OF COURSE!"

Beth always came over for the first Packers game of the season. They were playing their archrivals: the

Minnesota Vikings.

"Only Mom says I can't spend the night 'cause it's a school night."

She'd forgotten about that. Their parents were usually more lenient on first game night. Just one more reason why going to school was the worst.

Beth looked down and kicked at the asphalt.

"It's okay," Hannah said. "We'll still have fun."

"Yeah. I'll see you then?"

"See you then."

Hannah rubbed one foot on the other leg, hugging her towel to her. The heat seeped into her skin as she watched the Singleton's SUV pull away.

It was okay. Even if she couldn't spend the night, Beth still got to come to the game.

It would be okay.

And the first park day was only a week away. She would meet someone new. Someone who would keep park day and co-op from being unbearably boring.

CHAPTER 4

*H*annah's legs wouldn't move. It was like walking *through jelly. She had to get to the end zone. Just a few more steps. Just a few more—*

Bring! Bring!

Was that the phone? Hannah opened her eyes. The clock said six something a.m.

Bring! Bring!

She rolled over and stuffed the pillow in her ears. Dad's business partners shouldn't call so early.

"Hannah!" Mom's voice rang down the hall. She did not sound happy. "The phone!"

Hannah reached up for the portable on her headboard. She couldn't think of anyone who would call this early.

She clicked the phone on. "Hello?"

"Hannah? It's me!"

"Beth!" She sat straight up, her heart pounding. Maybe Beth's parents had decided not to put her in school!

"I'm getting ready for school, and I'm freaking out."

Hannah sank back into her warm pillows.

So much for that wish.

"We have orientation today. Do you know what orientation is?"

She shook her head. "No. What is it?"

"Mom says they'll show us around the school and give us our schedules and stuff. What if I can't find my class? Or . . . or miss it completely?"

Beth sounded so nervous. Her voice was fast and shaky. She was never nervous. Usually, Beth was the one calming *her* down.

Hannah looked around her room, searching for something reassuring to say. Her whole room made her think of Beth: the Green Bay Packers poster on the wall above the bed, the autographed football on her dresser. The corkboard above the desk was full of pictures of her and Beth wearing their jerseys at park day, doing science experiments, holding half a craw-dad in dissection class. Hannah even had a cheesehead that Beth had brought her.

Beth had actually been to a Packers game. *Lucky.*

She'd gotten lost in the stadium, but even then she hadn't panicked. Panicking was not like Beth.

Hannah had to say something. "You'll be fine. Just—just pretend it's co-op!"

Beth sighed into the phone. "Yeah. Okay. Want to meet at the park after school?"

"Sure! I want the postgame report."

Hannah hung up and snuggled back into her covers. She couldn't imagine getting up this early every day for school. That was ridiculous. She didn't start school for another week, and even when she did, she wouldn't have to get up *this* early.

Mom opened the hall door, and light poured over Hannah. She wore an apron over her robe, and her hair was pulled into a messy ponytail. A yummy cooking smell flowed into the room, hot and thick.

"Since we're already up," Mom said in her 'don't-mess-with-mom' voice, "we might as well be productive. I wanted to clean the schoolroom today anyway. Breakfast in half-an-hour."

Hannah threw the covers over her head and groaned. If Mom was going to start using a private school schedule, she might as well put her in school.

Hey, that's a thought.

Hannah pushed the covers down and sat up. If she could go to school, she'd be with Beth. She'd have someone to hang out with, someone on the same schedule. And there had to be more kids who liked the Packers at Beth's school. Maybe they could have a whole gang of friends, the way they used to. Of course, she'd have to get up at six a.m. every morning.

It would be worth it.

She was still thinking about it as the family sat down to waffles at the kitchen table. Everyone, including Dad. Usually, he left for work before the others were up. Dad wore his button-down business shirt and tie, but his sleeves were rolled up, and he was grinning like when they were on vacation.

She looked at the rest of her family. Mom still had her 'grumpy-to-be-up-so-early' face on, but it smoothed into a smile after another sip of coffee. Zach was way too energized for this time of the morning. He spread about a pound of butter on his waffles. Olivia didn't seem to mind being up so early. She was young enough that she still got naps sometimes.

"Syrup, please!" She raised her hands and reached for the bottle.

Dad glanced around the table. "Maybe we should make this a habit."

Hannah bit into her waffle, crusty hot on the outside and steamy soft inside. *Just right*. They normally had cold cereal for breakfast. Maybe getting up this early was worth it. If she went to school, maybe they'd do this more.

Hannah braced herself for a tackle and said, "This is fun. I think I'd like to get up this early every day."

Mom stared. Dad grinned.

"Don't say that!" Zach kicked her under the table.

Okay, Hannah had the ball, and the field was clear. She just had to wait for her opportunity.

CHAPTER 5

Today was the day to switch the family room from a play and art room back to a schoolroom. The yearly change always took a while. Mom cleared her desk of papers and brought the three kids' desks back from the garage to the middle of the room.

Hannah cleaned poster paints off the tile and wiped down the whiteboard. She thought about what Beth was doing right then: what classes were like and what was it like to have teachers. Teachers who weren't your mom.

Next she cleaned out her desk of last year's junk. She found broken pencils, an eraser shaped like a soccer ball, some silly putty that was hard as a rock. She was almost done when she spotted a crumpled piece of paper stuck in the back corner. Reaching her arm all the way into the desk, she worked the paper out with her fingers. It was an unfinished note to Beth.

Beth,
Can't wait to see you Friday!

She and Beth used to write each other notes all the time, especially when they were supposed to be doing school. They'd fold them into paper footballs and shoot them at each other during co-op on Fridays.

The words on the page blurred into the blue lines.

Middle schoolers don't cry.

Hannah crumpled the note for the trash bin. Maybe Beth wouldn't have time to write her notes anymore.

The doorbell rang.

"New books are here!" Mom called. She came into the schoolroom scooting a box in front of her. Hannah ran over with Zach and Olivia.

"Yay!" Olivia clapped her hands. This was her first real year of school, so of course, she was excited.

Hannah was a little excited, too. She liked seeing her new books and cracking their bindings. That always made Zach jealous. Except for workbooks, he had to use her old books. And besides, this was the first year of middle school. She'd be doing all kinds of new things.

As Zach slit into the box with his pocket knife, the smell of new books burst out. Hannah reached into the packing peanuts and pulled out a thin, glossy workbook. Olivia's 'learn the alphabet' book. Olivia squealed and grabbed the book from her. Hannah reached in again. This time, she scored her science book. The cover was green and had a photo of a lab table with beakers and test tubes and one of those flame stove things. The binding gave a satisfying crack as she opened the cover. The pages were smooth and full of color pictures, squiggly diagrams, and lots of experiments.

Mom pulled out other things: American History, Let's Do Math!, Cultures of the World, an experiment kit. Hannah's eyes widened as Mom stacked more and more books in front of her. This year would be hard, but it would be interesting, too.

Hannah grabbed the experiment kit and ripped into it. From the looks of the beakers and test tubes, she'd be getting into some chemistry this year. Maybe she'd even get to blow something up.

She had to call Beth!

Hannah was halfway to the phone before she remembered. She stopped and looked down at her feet.

Beth was at school.

There wasn't anyone to do experiments with.

She turned around. Zach had picked up her experiment kit and was looking at the beakers. Could she do experiments with him? *Not likely*. He was ages behind her in science.

Hannah sat back down by her stack of books. There had to be someone new in the homeschool group this year, someone she could do experiments with. Of course, if she was at Beth's school, they could keep doing experiments together, just like always.

Hannah took a deep breath and swallowed hard. She had been playing college ball too long. It was time to go pro. She'd rather suffer through getting up at six in the morning than have no one to hang out with.

Time for a new play.

"Mom?" Hannah forced her voice to be steady. "Are you sure you can handle all this?"

"What do you mean?" Mom asked without looking up from the packing list in her hand.

Hannah tapped the books in front of her. "This is complicated stuff. I mean, look at this." She pulled the math book from the bottom of the pile and flipped it open. "I'm starting geometry and pre-algebra. And look at this!" Hannah waved the science book in Mom's face. "I'm getting into chemistry and anatomy. I even saw a section in here on puberty. Are you sure you're up for all that?"

Mom raised an eyebrow. "I taught high school,

Hannah. I think I can handle puberty."

"I'm just saying, you might want to leave this to the professionals."

Mom rubbed her nose between her eyes. "I am a professional, Hannah. Even if I weren't, I could teach you this."

Skirting the edges wasn't working. Time to head straight down the field.

"Who am I going to do experiments with?" Hannah jiggled the experiment kit for emphasis.

"Ah. This is about Beth."

Of course, it's about Beth!

"I need someone to do science with." Hannah got to her knees and clasped her hands under her chin. "Can I pleeeeeeeeease go to school with Beth?"

"You know we can't afford a private school."

"Just return these books. I'm sure they'll give you a full refund if they're unused."

Mom sighed. "Returning the books won't pay tuition to a private school, and you need books whatever school you go to anyway."

"Then I'll go to public school!" A lot of Hannah's other friends were in public school. At least she'd already know people. "Half my friends are at King Middle already."

Honestly, Mom should be excited about this.

She'd have less work if Hannah went to school.

That's the whole reason Beth had to go to school in the first place.

"Wouldn't you like more free time?"

Olivia looked from Mom to Hannah. "I want to go to school."

Mom gave Hannah the 'now-see-what-you've-done' look.

"Dad has a good job that allows me to stay home with you guys. We should be thankful we have this opportunity."

"Well, I'm not." Hannah crossed her arms.

"Hannah." Mom's voice was serious. "Tell me honestly, would you enjoy being in a classroom from eight to three every day and having homework in the evenings?"

Hannah smiled as big as she could. "If I could pass notes with my friends."

"Honey, school isn't a hang out party. You wouldn't get to spend all day with your friends. You'd be doing schoolwork. You'd have a schedule assigned to you, and you probably wouldn't even have classes with your friends. It's not like co-op."

Hannah glared at the books in front of her. They didn't look so fun anymore. Not by herself. If she went to school, at least she'd be with her friends doing school instead of sitting in the schoolroom with no one but Zach and Olivia for company.

"You'll still get to see Beth," Mom said.

Hannah had missed some paint on the tile. She chipped at it with her toenail.

"You'll make new friends this year." Mom began to sound desperate. "Remember, last year Victoria joined the homeschool group?"

"For one year, and she didn't play sports."

Still, Mom was right. There were always new kids. Someone new *had* to have joined this year, too.

Hannah had heard of parents who sent their kids to public school for elementary, and then home-schooled for middle school and high school. Maybe there would be a bunch of new middle schoolers this year. Surely one of them would like sports. She'd even take a baseball fan or . . . or a golf fan if she had to.

Mom glanced at her watch. "Alright, kids, put your books on my desk so I can make the lesson plans. Then get your shoes. We'd better get moving if we're going to meet the Singletons at the park."

Coach blew the whistle. "Time out. That was a foul, Taylor."

"No, it wasn't." Hannah hadn't done anything wrong.

"You're out the rest of the game."

"What? First, you shove me onto the practice squad, and then you don't even let me practice?"

"I said, sit down!"

Hannah threw the ball into the ground. Beth and the

other starting players were still practicing, even though she'd been taken out of the game.

Bad call, Mrs. Singleton.

Bad call, Mom.

CHAPTER 6

Hannah opened the door before the van had even stopped.

"Hannah!" Mom jerked the vehicle into park. "You know better!"

"Sorry!" She jumped out and scanned the park for Beth. The sun cast a yellow tinge on the trees, and the birds sent up a chorus, as though they had just gotten out of school, too. A warm summer breeze blew gently through the grass.

Mom came around to where Hannah stood. "You need to set a good example for your siblings."

Olivia climbed out of the van with bright eyes. Everything was always about them.

"I'll do better," she muttered so Mom wouldn't start a lecture.

She spotted the Singleton's SUV a little way down

the parking lot. Beth was just climbing out. "Beth!"

Beth came running, her football tucked under her arm. She jumped into Hannah's left shoulder.

"Left side!"

"Strong side!"

Hannah laughed. This felt just like normal, but it wasn't quite. She almost didn't want to ask, but she had to know. "So—how was it?"

"It was awful!" Beth slumped her shoulders forward.

Of course it was.

They headed to their favorite clearing for throwing passes.

"Everybody kept asking me weird questions all day, stuff like, 'what did you used to do all day?' and 'didn't you hate doing school with your little siblings?' So I told them how we hang out all the time and watch the Packers and do science and have co-op and park days." Beth's eyes brightened.

Hannah took the football and backed up. Moving her fingers along the football's bumpy surface, she felt for the laces.

"I tried to talk my mom into letting me go to school with you." She hurled the ball.

Beth caught it without even moving. "And? What did she say?"

Beth sounded so hopeful. Maybe she shouldn't

34

have mentioned it. She dodged to the right to catch the ball as Beth threw it back. "A bunch of stuff about not being able to afford private school and how I'd never see you anyway and that I'd hate the homework."

"So, she didn't go for it?" Beth caught the ball, spun, and threw it without stopping.

"No." Hannah threw the ball with more force than she had meant to. Beth caught it with an 'oomph.'

They did a few more passes in silence. She wasn't so sure Mom was telling the truth about the money thing. She still might be able to convince her, but she shouldn't get Beth's hopes up. Poor Beth. She was stuck in school no matter what.

Beth wandered into the locker room where Hannah sat on the bench taking off her pads.

"How was the rest of practice?" Hannah asked.

Beth sat down and took off her helmet. "You should be glad you're just on the practice squad. Coach is working us too hard. I don't know if I can keep this up."

"Sure you can." Hannah punched Beth's shoulder pads. "You're Beth Singleton, the best quarterback in the whole NFL."

Beth smiled. "I just wish you were a starter this year."

"Well, you could still throw the ball in someone's face."

Beth laughed.

It was good to hear Beth laugh.

CHAPTER 7

Hannah sat down at her desk and pulled out her schoolbooks. She ran her fingers over the smooth pages and glossy covers. She'd always been excited on the first day of school. She knew from experience that the excitement wore off soon enough, but it usually lasted at least a week. Today, she just felt nervous.

Beth wouldn't be there at park day to eat sandwiches with, to share dessert with, to throw passes with.

But someone new would be.

And maybe the someone new would be an amazing football player. Maybe she'd love the Packers even more than Hannah did.

She twisted her hands around her pencil.

Maybe she wouldn't like Hannah.

Concentrating on school wasn't working. She read her literature passage twice and misspelled half the words on her spelling lesson. She stared at the math book on the desk in front of her until the words floated across the page. Blinking them back into focus, she reread the same problem she'd been on for half-an-hour.

"Everybody to the car!" Mom called.

Hannah jumped. It couldn't be lunchtime already! She heard Zach and Olivia scrambling toward the garage. They'd already finished their school.

She didn't move.

Mom appeared in the doorway. "Hannah, time to go."

"Already? But I haven't finished my math yet. I've still got science, too." Hannah's stomach swirled. If she could just concentrate, she'd be done by now. "I guess I can't go to the park today. It's your rule."

Mom tried to hide a smile. "Since your school is so complicated now that you're in sixth grade, we're changing the rule. You can come to park day and finish your school when we get home."

The blood drained from Hannah's head into her toes.

She can't change the rules mid-game. That's illegal.

That meant Hannah would have to do school after

park day while Zach and Olivia were playing. "But I'll have to do school until supper!"

"You wanted to know what homework was like."

Moms can be so heartless.

"Mom, this stuff is hard."

"I can help you when we get home. Now get your shoes."

"But I didn't make my sandwich."

Mom had an annoying twinkle in her eyes. "I made one for you."

The twisting in Hannah's stomach got worse, making her feel she never wanted to see a sandwich, or any other food, again.

She put her book into her desk and went out to the van. She paused with her hand on the door. "Can Beth spend the night this Friday?"

Mom shut the lunch cooler in the backseat with Zach and Olivia.

"Only if you quit stalling and get in the car."

Hannah climbed in and yanked the door closed.

There would be someone new today. Someone who would love sports and the Packers.

There had to be.

CHAPTER 8

The van went down the familiar tree-lined road to the park. Hannah's heart beat extra quick. Maybe the new friend would like basketball instead of football. Or maybe she'd like football but wouldn't like the Packers.

Well, Hannah could deal with that. At this point, she might even accept a Vikings fan as a friend—although that was asking a lot.

Hannah surveyed the vehicles as they pulled into the gravel parking lot. There was the car of Zach's best friend. There were a few cars of the moms with little kids who were Olivia's friends. There was the Singleton's SUV.

Mrs. Singleton was still homeschooling the

younger kids. That just wasn't fair. They shouldn't come to park day if they weren't going to bring Beth.

But there weren't any unfamiliar vehicles.

This is impossible!

No one new had joined.

Mom had practically promised someone new would be at park day. Hannah's heart pounded. She couldn't throw passes by herself.

Olivia unbuckled, squealed, and ran off. *Lucky.* Kids that age always have plenty of friends. Parents don't send their little kids to school.

As Hannah got out of the van with her football, the gravel crunched under her feet. The air was still warm with summer heat. Robins chirped in the tall oaks as if this were just another normal park day. But it wasn't a normal park day.

No one new had come.

Something poked Hannah in the ribs. She turned to see Zach aiming his empty dart gun at her.

"Ah! Grumpy Monkey is after me!" he shouted and ran off.

Hannah scooped up the dart and hurled it after him. "Get lost!"

"Hannah," Mom said in a warning voice. She put her hand on Hannah's shoulder. "I know you're frustrated that Beth isn't here, but don't take it out on your siblings." She smiled. "It looks like the Smiths and the Poles are here. They have girls about your age. Why don't you see if you can find them?"

Hannah kicked at the gravel, sending a shower into the van's tires. This wasn't fair. 'About your age' was Mom's way of saying 'they have girls way younger than you, but that's the closest you're going to get.'

There was supposed to be someone new here today. Someone her age.

No one new had come.

Hannah took her lunch from Mom and found an empty table away from everybody. She pulled her sandwich, juice, and pretzels out of the brown bag and imagined Beth sitting at a lunch table in a cafeteria all by herself missing Hannah just as much as she missed her. Was she eating a turkey sandwich, too?

Hannah slowly munched and swallowed each bite. It didn't taste as good without a friend to talk to.

Laughter erupted from the playground. Hannah turned and saw a group of girls squealing at the merry-go-round. They were the ballerinas from the pool party, and they looked like they were playing pony or something. Those were the girls *about* Hannah's age. She shuddered and looked back at her pretzels.

She had to find *someone* to hang out with. Zach and his friends were out of the question. She would not stoop to playing with her little brother.

Most of the high schoolers played sports. Maybe

she could join them. Maybe they'd even play football.

She crumpled her trash into the brown bag and chucked it into the trash can.

Looking around the park, she spotted the high schoolers. They were over in that big field where she and Beth used to throw passes with all their friends.

Back when she had friends.

Hannah grabbed her football and headed that way.

Being newly drafted was scary. Yeah, she'd been picked up by the Packers, but she was only on the practice squad. What right did she have to ask all these pros to a game? She forced herself forward. Her new Green Bay jersey gave her confidence.

"Wanna play?"

The pros all turned to look at her. Their eyebrows squished together, and they glared.

The quarterback frowned and spun the ball in his hand. "Why don't you play with the practice squad?" He didn't have to act so superior. He was only the backup quarterback for Beth.

"They're injured," Hannah said.

"What about them?" He pointed to the pony-playing ballerina girls.

Hannah stared at him. He couldn't be serious. "That isn't a football team." It wasn't any kind of a sports team.

The quarterback shrugged like it wasn't his problem.

Completely ignoring her, the players turned back to their game.

She should have known the pros wouldn't play with her. She was just a rookie on the practice squad.

But she was good at football. She ought to be more than just a practice squad rookie.

This wasn't fair.

Hannah closed her eyes and turned away.

If no one else would play with her, she'd just have to practice on her own.

Hannah tucked the ball under her arm for their trick play. The game was nearly over, and they were down by six points. She was their only chance! The defensive lineman bore down on her, about to tackle.

Think fast!

She saw a group of her teammates, free and clear. She raised her hand and threw the ball hard in the most amazing lateral pass in Green Bay history. It soared through the air.

Look up, look up!

"INCOMING!"

The players looked up—then shrieked and ran.

Hannah walked over to where the ballerina girls had been a moment before to retrieve her ball. She'd hoped that at least one of them would know how to catch a football. Hannah raised her eyebrows at their cute pastel T-shirts and equally cute pastel shorts.

43

Maybe not.

One of the girls stalked toward Hannah. She shouldn't be intimated by a pony-playing ballerina, but this girl towered over the other girls, including her. The giant couldn't be any older than ten, but her height made her seem like a middle schooler.

"Are you trying to murder us?" the giant asked.

Hannah balanced the ball on her hip.

Throwing passes by herself obviously wasn't going to work.

She glanced around as the girls trickled back toward their leader, some with hands over their hearts. They were only a year or two younger than she was.

It couldn't hurt to ask.

"Does anyone want to throw passes with me?"

The giant tossed her thick hair. "I don't know *what* you mean, but I'm sure it would be beneath the dignity of a princess."

All the pony-playing ballerinas stood in a circle around Hannah and the giant. Except for one. She was the only one who hadn't run when the football landed in the middle of them. She hung upside down from the monkey bars, her dusty blond hair skimming the bits of chopped-up tire beneath her. She waved.

"Where are your friends?" asked a girl with thick, poofy hair.

"They're all at school this year."

Thanks for rubbing it in.

The girls exchanged glances as if Hannah's bad luck might rub off on them.

The upside-down girl flipped over and came up to her. Grabbing the edges of an invisible skirt, she curtsied. "I'm Alexis. How do you do?"

Hannah raised her eyebrows. "I'm Hannah."

"Want to play with us?" Alexis sounded eager, as though she really wanted her to, which was at least more than the high schoolers had done.

Hannah took a deep breath. She wasn't sure she was bored enough. It depended completely on what they were playing.

Alexis shifted into the circle of girls, leaving room for her.

"What princess color are you?" the giant demanded.

"What?"

"What—princess—color—are—you?" The girl emphasized each word as if Hannah weren't smart enough to understand.

Great. They were playing princess. That was even worse than pony. She clutched the football to her chest.

"Do you have a princess color?" asked Alexis. Her voice danced.

Hannah shook her head. She didn't even know

what a princess color was. Alexis and some of the girls squealed.

"Then we can help you pick one!" Alexis clapped her hands together, her eyes shining.

CHAPTER 9

That wasn't so bad, was it?" Mom asked as they pulled away from the park.

Hannah glared out the window. "Beth gets to come over twice now."

"It couldn't have been that bad."

She scrunched down in her seat.

"My princess color is pink."

CHAPTER 10

"I'll get it!" Hannah shouted when the doorbell rang. She flung open the door and pulled Beth inside. "I am so happy to see you!"

"Me too!"

Beth slung her arm around Hannah's shoulders and squeezed.

Hannah stiffened. That wasn't a normal jumping-up-and-down tackle-hug. It was some kind of one-arm wimpy-hug.

"It feels like forever!" Beth said.

"I know! It's wild." Hannah thumped Beth's back, just like old times. No wimpy-hugs from her. "Come on. Mom's got supper ready."

"What do you think of the Packers' starting lineup this year?" Beth asked as they walked to the dining room.

"I'm excited about the new wide receiver. I bet he's gonna be great."

"Me, too."

They sat down to chili dogs and soda, their traditional first game meal.

"How's school, Beth?" Mom cut Olivia's hot dog into tiny pieces.

"Okay, I guess, but I have a test next week." Beth turned to Hannah. "Can you believe I completely forgot about tests?"

"You forgot?" Tests were the worst part of any school.

Beth laughed. "I know. Weird, right? But Mom's tests were always more like discussions. Sometimes I didn't even realize she was testing me. I'm kind of glad now my mom is such a harsh grader."

"Sh!" Hannah did not need Mom to have new ammunition the next time she complained about her grading.

Dad passed Beth the chili. "How are your classes?"

Beth winked at Hannah. Maybe she still thought Mom and Dad might put Hannah in school, too. "Well, history would be boring, but we've got the most fun teacher. He talks like he was actually there." To Hannah, she whispered, "He's so old, he probably was."

Hannah snickered into her soda.

"Math class is hard, but we have an awesome teacher. She makes the problems into a game."

Beth's face brightened as she went on. She was really good at acting. She sounded as though she actually enjoyed school.

"And the food is fun 'cause we get french fries every day."

Hannah kicked Beth under the table.

"Sorry, I meant on Fridays. The rest of the time, the food is pretty nutritious and boring." Beth put some potato chips on her plate. "Gym class is fun 'cause we get to play different sports and games and stuff." She turned to Hannah. "You'd love it."

Beth didn't seem like she was acting. Maybe she was just making the best of it. If she were making the best of school, it might sound as though she enjoyed it.

That must be it.

Hannah bit into her hot dog, but it didn't taste quite as good as usual. Beth got to eat french fries every day and play sports and games with a whole class of kids her age.

"And every Friday we have an assembly that should be boring, but we make it fun."

Hannah looked at Beth.

Who is 'we?'

As if she were wondering the same thing, Mom asked, "Have you made any friends yet?"

Mom shouldn't ask that question. Of course Beth hadn't made any friends. She'd only been there like two weeks.

But Beth said, "No," a little too quickly and glanced at Hannah, almost guiltily. She took a huge bite of her chili dog.

Beth couldn't have made a friend already.

"So," Beth slowly continued. "My school is so small that everyone has to play sports for them to have full teams." She looked at Hannah, then looked away. She wanted Hannah to say something.

"What does that mean?"

"Well." Beth looked down at her plate. "I have to play on the volleyball team."

Play on the volleyball . . . *what?*

Mom smiled. "That's great, Beth."

Dad gave her a high five. "Let us know when you have a game, and we'll come cheer you on."

Mom and Dad didn't understand. This was terrible. Beth wasn't supposed to play sports without Hannah. *They* were a team—they always played together.

She had wanted to tell Beth about park day and the ballerina girls and playing princess because there was nothing else to do, but now . . .

Could Beth be enjoying school?

Beth wanted her approval; that's what those looks

meant. She wanted Hannah to be excited.

Hannah tried to smile. "That's awesome."

She didn't want to talk about school anymore. Maybe the more she had Beth over, the more Beth would forget about school.

"Before I forget," Hannah said. "Want to come over this Friday? Mom said twice in one week would be okay since you can't spend the night tonight and 'cause we don't get to see each other at park day, and then we could get ready for the Sunday game." She paused to take a breath, but she didn't want to stop talking. She didn't want to give Beth the chance to answer because Beth looked more and more uncomfortable.

"I can't."

Hannah glanced at Mom for help. "Maybe if my mom talked to your mom . . ." She sounded desperate.

Stop sounding desperate.

Hannah clenched her fists. She had to get ahold of herself.

"No, I mean I can't." Beth finally met Hannah's eyes. "There's a meeting. For volleyball."

There was no way there would be a meeting on a Friday.

"Maybe you could come over afterward?" Hannah tried to sound casual, like it was no big deal.

"It goes pretty late."

"Oh. Okay."

Fine. Whatever.

They couldn't have mandatory meetings on Friday nights. It must be an optional meeting. If it was optional, Beth could choose not to go.

Zach jumped out of his chair. "The game's starting!"

Hannah sighed in relief. The game was something normal, something real. She glanced at Beth to see what she'd do.

Beth dropped her chili dog and ran to the living room.

Just like old times.

Hannah grinned and ran after her, vaulting onto the couch.

"Who do you think will win tonight?" She asked. A true fan always thought the Packers would win, no matter what. "The Vikings? They have a good team this year."

"No way!" Beth shook her head. "They don't have a chance."

Hannah grinned.

Good.

All she had to do was to keep Beth focused on the game and the Packers. Make her forget about school and tests and volleyball and all that. For the next two hours, it was just Beth, Hannah, and the Packers.

Hannah crouched over the ball and waited for Beth to give the signal. She waited. And waited. Coach blew the whistle. The play clock had run out. Hannah stood up and turned around. Beth was staring off into the stands, not even paying attention to practice. Hannah shoved her shoulder.

"Wake up, QB. We have to practice or we'll never be ready for the next game."

Beth shook her head. "Oh yeah, sorry."

"Singleton!" Coach yelled.

Beth cringed.

"Are you going to play or are you going to stand there all day staring at the clouds?"

"She's ready," Hannah called. "Come on, Beth," she whispered. "Get your head in the game."

"Right." Beth held her hands out, ready to receive the snap.

Maybe the pressure of being the starting quarterback was getting to her.

CHAPTER 11

Hannah was working on 'varying your sentence structure' when Mom came into the school-room and announced, "Time to pick co-op classes!"

Hannah's stomach flipped. She told it to calm down. Co-op was usually the best part of the school year. Getting up every Friday to spend the morning with friends, taking fun classes for three hours, and then usually going to lunch or spending the afternoon at someone's house. One of the best parts was that Mom would let them off doing their normal school for the day.

Hannah and Beth had always picked classes together.

"Yay!" Olivia dropped her book and clapped. Of course, Olivia was too young to actually pick classes.

For her age group, there was just one class an hour.

Hannah set down her pencil and closed her book. She twisted her legs together and apart again, then together. If they offered just one good class this year, co-op might be bearable.

"They'd better have good classes for boys this time." Zach crossed his arms.

Mom sat at her desk and consulted the paper. "We do try."

Hannah squeezed her hands together until her fingers turned white. Mom read the list out loud, starting with Olivia's classes. She got Music, Art, and Story Time. Zach's classes didn't sound too bad. He picked Dissection, Drama, and Spanish.

Hannah held her breath as Mom read the list of classes for her age group.

First hour was Doll Making, Crochet, or Learn Spanish through Song.

Second hour was Ladies of Distinction or Gentlemen of Character.

Third hour was Science or Games.

Coach read off a list of plays and showed the charts to the practice squad.

"This is what we'll be running at next practice. I want everybody on their best game."

Hannah grabbed the charts from Coach and stared at them. This was ridiculous. These weren't plays. They were baby things. Dances. Wimpy stuff. She couldn't possibly do any of these plays.

This huddle was over.

Zach looked from Hannah to Mom. "Wow, Hannah, those classes are dumb."

Olivia gasped. "Momma, he said—"

"Watch your language, Zachery."

Hannah pounded her fists on the desk. "But those classes are dumb!"

"Hannah."

"I just won't go to co-op this year. I'm not doing it." None of those classes were even remotely interesting, and there wouldn't be anyone in class she could be miserable with.

"Oh, come on." Mom smiled. "It will be good for you to try some new things. You might find something else you enjoy as much as sports and science."

As if there could be anything as much fun as sports and science.

She sighed. Mom would probably make her do her normal schoolwork if she stayed home anyway. She had to grit her teeth or suffer through math and grammar home alone on a Friday.

Well, maybe she hadn't heard right. Maybe the classes weren't as bad as they first sounded.

Please, please let them be not as bad as they first sounded.

Closing her eyes, Hannah said, "What are my first hour choices again? Girly, really girly, and Spanish?"

"Doll Making—"

Hannah's eyes shot open. "What is Doll Making? Who makes dolls?" Hannah wrapped her feet around the legs of her desk. The metal was cold on her bare skin.

Olivia and Zach watched with rapt attention, waiting for the explosion. Mom waved at them to leave.

Mom grimaced, looking back at the paper. "Take Learn Spanish through Song, then."

"I am not singing. And I already speak Spanish! ¡Perfectamente!"

"Your only other option is Crochet."

"Are you serious?" Hannah dropped her head onto the desk.

"Crocheting can be fun." Mom was trying too hard.

"If you have gray hair and a cat on your lap."

"Lots of people crochet." Mom rubbed her nose between her eyes. "You have to pick something."

Hannah was definitely not taking Doll Making; that was for sure. And she'd be bored out of her mind in Learn Spanish through Song, especially if she didn't know anyone in the class. At least Crochet wouldn't be as silly as Doll Making or as boring as Spanish.

"Fine. I'll take Crochet. What's next?"

Mom consulted the list. "You don't have a choice second hour. The only two classes are Ladies of Distinction and Gentlemen of Character, which is a boys-only class."

Hannah raised her head. "*What* is Ladies of Distinction?"

"The description says it's a class to help girls grow into young women." Mom did not sound nearly disgusted enough.

"Whose idea was that?"

"Mrs. Robinski. She's the one teaching it anyway."

Hannah gave up hope for anything good and sank back in her chair. "What do I get third hour?"

"Oh!" Mom sounded entirely too cheerful. "You can take Experiments in Earth Science third hour. You love science."

"Mom!" Mom didn't understand *anything*. She was not doing science without Beth. And they'd already done earth science. Besides, "Why would I do normal school on a Friday?"

"You would do normal school every Friday if you went to public school."

Hannah was beginning to equate Mom with the Minnesota Vikings—Arch Nemesis Number One. "What's my other choice?"

"Games."

"Games, of course! Like outdoor ones?"

Mom looked down at the paper crinkling in her hand. "Like board ones."

Olivia peeped around the door where she had obviously been listening. She held up her smelly stuffed rabbit. "You could take music with me, Hannah. Don't you want to be in class with me and Fluffy?"

Hannah pounded her head on the desk.

"Well," Mom said, sounding as exasperated as she should have sounded reading off that list of classes. "Now that we've all picked classes, let's go get the supplies. Come on, get your shoes on."

"You need supplies to grow into a young woman?"

"Hannah, come on."

Groaning, she got to her feet and went to find her shoes.

CHAPTER 12

An entire wall of yarn faced Hannah. Bright pinks and purples dared her to buy them. She ran her fingers down the rows. Some yarns were soft and light while others were scratchy and rough. One kind was made out of leather. She had no idea what to pick.

"Mom!" she yelled.

Mom came around the corner with the cart. Olivia sat in the seat clutching her stuffed rabbit.

"I'm right here."

Hannah craned her head back. The yarn went all the way to the ceiling. "Which yarn do I get?"

Mom pulled the co-op paper out of her purse and skimmed it. "It says to get two colors, one skein each, and try to find DK yarn."

Hannah squinted at the yarn in front of her. "What is DK yarn?"

Mom flipped the page over, looking for more. "I'm not sure."

The Crochet teacher ought to explain what DK yarn was. This was supposed to be a learning experience.

Hannah rubbed some yarn between her fingers. It didn't really matter what she picked since she didn't want to learn crochet anyway.

"I want this one, Momma," Olivia said. She grabbed a skein of soft baby yarn.

Hannah picked a skein of yellow and a skein of green. She held them next to each other. "What do you think? Do they say 'Packer' to you?"

Mom smiled. "Sure do."

"Catch, Olivia!" Hannah threw the green yarn football style. Olivia opened her arms for it but missed. The yarn went straight into her eye. She screamed.

"Hannah!" Mom scolded.

Hannah hurried over as Olivia burst into tears. "I wasn't trying to hit her, I promise." She scooped up the green yarn from where it had fallen to the ground.

Mom wiped Olivia's cheeks with a tissue. "You're okay, honey."

"Hannah!" someone shouted from the end of the aisle.

Maybe Beth was out shopping too!

Hannah spun around. *No, of course not.* Beth was in school.

That girl from the park, the super friendly one—Alexis—came down the aisle with her mom and little sister.

"We're buying our co-op supplies." Alexis looked at the yarn in Hannah's hands. "Are you taking Crochet, too? What other classes are you taking?"

Hannah looked to Mom for help. Mom read off the paper. "Crochet, Ladies of Distinction, and Games."

Alexis' eyes got big. "Me, too!"

They were in the same age group? Hannah poked the wheel of the cart with her toe. Of course they were. No middle schoolers were in the homeschool group anymore. She had probably been dumped in with the fourth and fifth graders. No wonder the class selection stank.

"I'm excited about Crochet," Alexis went on. "My grandmother can crochet, and she made me a b*eau*tiful afghan. I hope I can be as good as she is." She tilted her head. "I thought your princess color was pink?"

Hannah looked at the yarn in her hands. No one had told her she was supposed to get her princess color. "Um, I just like these colors." She was pretty sure Alexis wouldn't understand team colors.

But Alexis nodded as if she did understand. She

looked longingly at a skein of yellow yarn.

"So, do you know what DK yarn is?" Hannah asked. She didn't want to crochet, but she also didn't want to look silly showing up with the wrong supplies.

"We asked my grandma." Alexis ran her fingers over the rows of the yarn. "It's the weight of the yarn. Grandma said the packages should say."

Hannah checked the label of her yarn. It said "worsted." *Great.* She'd picked the worst kind.

"Here's DK!" Alexis held up two skeins of yarn. They were different shades of purple. "I think they match, don't you?"

"What about that yellow?" Hannah pointed to the yarn Alexis had been eyeing a moment before.

"Oh. Well, my princess color is violet. And Lydia's is yellow."

Lydia—she was the giant, know-it-all girl. She couldn't have exclusive rights to the color yellow. This princess thing was complicated. Well, Hannah didn't care what the princesses thought; she was getting Packers colors.

She put back the worst yarn and with Alexis' help, found suitable substitutes in the DK section.

They moved to an aisle covered with metal hooks and plastic hooks and big huge needles and things that looked like torture devices. Thankfully, Mrs. Smith knew what to pick.

Alexis handed her yarn to her mom. "Ooh, Momma, can Hannah come with us to get ice cream?"

"Sure." Mrs. Smith placed the hooks in her basket.

Alexis grabbed Hannah's arm. "Come, Princess Ruby. Ice cream is a foreign delicacy that will boggle your mind." She turned to Mom before Hannah had a chance to say anything.

"Mrs. Taylor?"

Mom looked up from her grocery list.

"Yes?"

"Could Hannah come with us to get ice cream?"

Hannah tried desperately to signal Mom 'No, no, no!' without letting Alexis see.

Mom smiled. "That's a great idea."

Traitor.

Alexis skipped into the air. "This will be so much fun!" She ran off to where Mrs. Smith was examining sewing supplies.

Mom tucked her list into her pocket. "See Hannah, you're making friends."

Hannah rolled her eyes. "Didn't you get my signal?"

"You don't want to go?"

"And play princess all afternoon with a nine-year-old? Of course not!"

"I think she's about your age, Hannah. You might have a good time if you just tried."

Sure. And Detroit might win the Super Bowl.

Alexis came skipping back. "Come hither, Princess Ruby!"

Hannah gave Mom an I-told-you-so look. Mom just smiled and shooed her away.

Hannah turned to where Alexis was practically dancing with excitement. "I thought I was Princess Pink?"

Alexis linked arms with her. "Pink is too ordinary. Ruby is much more elegant."

Hannah sighed. Well, at least she wasn't Princess Pink anymore.

"I'm glad you're taking Games, too," said Alexis. "I thought about taking science, but who wants to do real school on a Friday?"

Hannah smiled, just a little.

She and Alexis had one thing in common anyway.

CHAPTER 13

The car stopped in front of an older house with a big tree in the front yard. A sidewalk led to a front porch surrounded by bushes and shrubs. Mrs. Smith pulled into the garage. When they climbed out, chewing the last of their ice cream cones, Hannah heard barking. Alexis opened the door to the house. A medium-sized brown mutt jumped up and licked at her hand.

"Down, Arthur! Don't be rude to our guest." She pulled him back. "Don't you think he looks like an Arthur? I thought about naming him Merlin, but he didn't seem very magical."

So, it was Arthur as in King Arthur. He didn't look very kingly either.

Hannah stepped inside and looked around. They'd

come into a small kitchen. A stack of dirty dishes sat by the sink, but other than that, it seemed pretty clean. Alexis led the way through the kitchen into the living room. The carpet was worn, and the brown couch looked old. A small, upright piano stood against one wall. The house smelled like warm towels.

"Want to see my room?"

Alexis turned into a narrow hallway. She opened a door onto a room smaller than Hannah's. Bunk beds stood against one wall. Two dressers lined the walls across from the bunk beds. A sliding door opened into a closet. Alexis climbed up to the top bunk and lay down.

"I sleep up here. Phoebe gets the lower bunk."

Hannah sat on the floor and looked up at her. The carpet was thin and unpadded. "Doesn't it annoy you to share with your little sister?"

Alexis shrugged. "Sometimes, but it can be fun, too. I like to pretend Phoebe is a lost princess and the fairies charged me with keeping her safe so she can ascend to the throne one day."

Hannah imagined pretending Olivia was a football. *That wouldn't end well.*

Alexis clasped her hands under her chin. "What would you like to do?"

Hannah looked around the room. She wasn't really sure what their options were. "I don't know. Wanna go outside and shoot some goals or something?"

Alexis sprang to her knees. "I love shooting! But I lent my bow to Emma, and I don't think she's given it back yet."

Oh, she meant with a bow and arrow. That wasn't exactly the kind of shooting Hannah had in mind.

"Do you have a football or a soccer ball or something?"

Alexis cocked her head. "I think there's a soccer ball in the garage. What did you want to do with it?"

"We could–" Hannah stopped before she said 'play soccer.' Maybe telling Alexis she wanted to play ball was a bad idea. There had to be something she could say that would make Alexis want to. Something princess. "We could pretend it's a cannon ball and kick it at the dragon."

That wasn't half bad.

Alexis clapped her hands. "That sounds like fun!"

Hannah raced down the field, dribbling the ball between her feet. She was better at football, but Coach thought soccer practice would help them with their footwork. Hannah just had to make it past the other team's defenders and score. The goal was in sight now. Just fake to the left, go to the right—

The goal suddenly shifted into a shining, green dragon. It reared its scaly head and blew fire right at Hannah. The heat burned her face. A girl dressed in a flowing purple gown screamed.

"Princess Ruby!"

She shoved Hannah aside and kicked the ball—which had turned hard and black—right into the dragon's mouth. With a pop, the dragon disappeared.

Hannah stayed where she was, lying on the ground. She propped herself on her elbows and looked up at Alexis. Her face was flushed, and she grinned.

"That was fun! I heard there's another dragon in the next kingdom over."

CHAPTER 14

Hannah pressed her nose against the window and watched houses come into focus as the van slowed and pulled into the church parking lot. This was it, the first day of co-op without Beth. The church seemed smaller this year, and there were a lot more little kids running around. As soon as the van stopped, Zach and Olivia were out and running toward the sanctuary.

Just wait until they were in middle school and had no friends.

Hannah pulled her backpack—real NFL-certified merchandise—onto her lap and hugged it close. Holding something Packers made Beth feel not so far away.

The team bus stopped in front of the stadium. This was Hannah's first away game since joining the team.

No big deal. She shouldn't be nervous, especially playing against a team with such a lousy record. The Packers would have no problem trouncing them. Still, she'd only been moved to the active roster for this game because they were short a player. QB Singleton couldn't make it today. Hannah surveyed the team. They were all nervous. This was also their first game without their star quarterback.

Mom opened Hannah's door. "You can't stay in the van all morning." She patted her shoulder. "Come on."

Hannah slid off her seat onto the asphalt. She trudged toward the building, kicking up gravel with her dragging feet. The school supplies and crochet stuff in her backpack felt as heavy as rocks. The straps dug into her shoulders, holding her back. If she didn't go inside, she wouldn't see that Beth wasn't there. She could pretend that this was a normal Friday.

Hannah turned toward the sound of laughter and saw the high schoolers grouped around an old car. They were chatting, laughing, texting. If she could just hang out with them. . . .

She remembered what had happened at the park and kept walking.

When she pushed open the sanctuary doors, a chorus of shouts met her ears. Bright lights hung from the ceiling by cords. Kids were everywhere. But no Beth.

This was going to be a long morning.

Pulling the straps of her backpack tighter, Hannah went to the corner where a high schooler manned the name tag table. She had just figured out the name tags were grouped by age rather than alphabetical order when arms wrapped around her neck, choking her, and someone yelled, "Hannah!" right in her ear. For a brief moment, Hannah thought it was Beth, but then she recognized Alexis' face amid the tangle of limbs.

"I'm so excited! Aren't you excited?" Alexis danced from foot to foot.

Hannah rubbed her throat and fought the sinking feeling in her chest. "About what?"

Of course it wasn't Beth.

Alexis rolled her eyes, still grinning. "About co-op, of course." Her smile lit up her whole face.

Hannah tried to smile back.

"Look! I decorated my name tag." Alexis pointed to the name tag on her shoulder. It was covered with purple swirls, and 'Alexis Smith' had been crossed out and replaced by 'Princess Violet' written in purple gel pen. "Want to do yours? I've got lots of colors, and I have a couple different kinds of red."

Alexis held up a lunch box covered in purple swirls. It rattled whenever she moved it. She set it on the table and opened it. Inside was overflowing with pens and pencils.

Hannah glanced around. She didn't have any friends here. All the kids running around playing together were younger. No one would care if she decorated her name tag.

Hannah shrugged. "Sure." She had nothing better to do. She wasn't doing swirls, though. Instead, she drew a big football in one corner and the Green Bay *G* in another.

Alexis picked up a schedule from the table. "Ooh! We have Crochet first. Let's sit together."

Hannah just had time to grab her name tag before Alexis linked arms with her and marched down the aisle.

At least she had someone to sit with.

They found the pew labeled 'Crochet' and sat down. Hannah scooted forward. She should have worn jeans, not shorts. The seat cushion had a pattern of dots on it, and the dots itched.

One of the princesses sat down next to Alexis and started talking with her. Kids were hurrying down the aisles to find their classes. The high schoolers sauntered in and sat in the back rows. One mom told some boys Zach's age to stop playing with the hymnals.

If Beth were here, she and Hannah would be outside throwing passes until the last possible minute or flicking paper footballs at each other across the aisle.

"I like your backpack." Alexis pointed at Hannah's

green bag. She smiled so big her eyes sparkled.

"Thanks." Hannah waved at Alexis' shiny metal box. "Cool lunch box."

When the co-op director told everyone to find their seats, Alexis turned her full attention to the front of the room. The noise gradually diminished while everyone settled down.

"Welcome to fall co-op!" said the director. "We're really excited about this year. I have just a few announcements, and then we'll dismiss you by class."

Hannah sighed and leaned her head against the pew. Announcements were the worst part. At least once they got to class they'd be doing something. Alexis already had her crochet hook out and was trying to figure out how to use it. Hannah sat on her hands to keep from fidgeting.

The youngest classes were dismissed first. When the kindergarten class filed down the aisle past the Crochet pew, Olivia held her stuffed rabbit under one arm and waved with the other. Hannah ignored her, pretending they weren't related.

Alexis waved and smiled. A little blond girl, her sister Phoebe, waved back. Phoebe smiled so big when her sister waved at her. Maybe Olivia would smile like that if Hannah waved. She looked down at her shoes.

After what seemed like ages, the director called out, "Crochet."

The class stood and followed a mom Hannah didn't recognize to one of the Sunday School rooms. A long table took up most of the room. Light from the one window illuminated dust motes in the air, and the room smelled comfortably old. Alexis pulled Hannah to a seat. They were a small class, just five. Everyone else must have taken Spanish. The kid who sat down across from Hannah was a boy. He looked as uncomfortable as she was. No, worse. At least she had Alexis.

The mom set down a bag with papers and yarn sticking out the top. She was one of the younger moms, with a nice haircut and a blazer over her top. She wasn't the kind of person Hannah would have pegged as a crochet teacher.

"Okay, everybody. Welcome to Crochet. Let's go around and introduce ourselves. I'm Mrs. Wells, Melissa's mom." She patted the shoulder of the girl next to her who said, "I'm Melissa." She had curly brown hair and was probably about ten. She was dressed nice, too.

"I'm Hannah."

"I am Alexis. Pleased to make your acquaintance." If she hadn't been sitting, Alexis probably would have curtsied.

The next girl was Princess Emerald. "I'm Emma." She leaned over to Alexis and Hannah. "The other princesses took Doll Making."

Thank goodness. At least for this hour, they

wouldn't have Lydia looking down her nose at them telling them all how unprincessy they were acting.

The boy shrugged his shoulders up to his ears, which were turning pink. "I'm Victor, and I'm only in this class 'cause I already speak Spanish, and I was no way making dolls."

Mrs. Wells smiled. "Lots of boys crochet, Victor. I made sure to bring some patterns for 'guy stuff.'"

She addressed the entire class next. "We're going to start simple. I have several projects. When you finish one, you can move on to a more advanced project. Today, we'll go over the basics and take it from there."

She passed around sheets with instructions and black and white illustrations. The pictures were fuzzy and hard to understand, and the page was full of weird phrases and abbreviations like 'yarn over' and 'SC1.' The abbreviation key didn't help much.

Hannah glanced around the room. The others had wrinkled foreheads or were chewing their lips. *Good.* At least everybody was as confused as she was.

They spent the rest of the hour learning how to hold the hook and the yarn and how to make loops. Crocheting was more complicated than she'd thought. Good thing Alexis had helped her pick the right yarn. She'd just begun to get the hang of it when a mom peeked her head in to say class was over. Hannah shoved the yarn into her bag.

"Practice this week," Mrs. Wells said as they lined up at the door. "We'll start on projects next week."

Their class joined the throng heading back to the sanctuary for assembly.

"There's Lydia and Morgan!" Emma waved so hard her arm should have fallen off. She brought her hand down quickly and looked at Hannah and Alexis apologetically. "I mean the Princesses Amber and Sapphire."

Alexis smiled at Emma. Hannah just shrugged. Aside from Lydia, who acted superior and took the lead on everything, Hannah couldn't remember who the girls were anyway, by their real names or their princess names. Lydia and Morgan joined them, and they filed into a pew together with all the other princesses.

Hannah looked up and saw Melissa Wells standing in the aisle.

"Can I sit here?" Melissa asked.

Hannah made room. "So, you're new here?"

"Sort of. We used to live outside of town, but the commute was hard on my dad. We live real close now, so we can actually come to co-op and stuff. We're going to start coming to park day, too."

Someone new *had* joined. Hannah looked at Melissa's new shoes and trendy sweater. She was still younger than Hannah, and her mom was the Crochet teacher. She probably wouldn't be any more interested in throwing passes than the princesses were.

Alexis leaned across Hannah. "Hi! I'm Alexis. Do you have a princess color?"

Melissa glanced at Hannah. "Um, no?"

"What's your favorite color?"

"Red?"

"That's already taken by Princess Ruby." Alexis beamed at Hannah. She gathered the other princesses, and they went through all the colors already taken: ruby, amber, emerald, sapphire, violet—pretty much the whole rainbow.

"I know!" Alexis squealed and clasped her hands. "You can be Princess Ebony."

Hannah frowned at her. She could have thought of Ebony when all the other princesses insisted on pink.

Ladies of Distinction was in one of the big fellowship rooms. Hannah and Alexis wound up at the end of the line as they filed in. This room was carpeted and was lit by fluorescent lights. Several round tables had been set up toward the other end.

"Oh, all the good seats are taken!" Alexis stopped and stared at the tables at the front, which were all full.

Hannah pulled out a chair at the table farthest back. "It's okay. We can sit here."

Alexis sighed, but she sat down.

Mrs. Robinski was a tall woman with a lot of hair. She stood at the front and clapped her hands. She was exactly the kind of person Hannah would expect to teach a class called Ladies of Distinction.

"Good morning, girls! I'm so excited to be here!"

From the murmurings around the room, all the other girls were, too. All of them except Hannah. If Beth were here, they could write notes to each other about how silly this class was and how annoying the girls were.

Ladies of Distinction was the most boring class that ever existed. Mrs. Robinski passed out folders with lots of pages about becoming young women. They were going to talk about self-image, clothes, hair, makeup, shaving, cooking, and all the stuff that didn't matter one smidgen to a football player.

Hannah tried to have a thumb war with Alexis, but she was paying too much attention. Instead, she hid her notebook under the table and started to write.

Dear Beth,
Life is terrible without you. The only girls to hang out with play princess. Co-op is so boring this year. While you're off having fun playing volleyball, I'm stuck learning how to shave my armpits.

Hannah crumpled the note and shoved it in

her bag. There was no point in writing to Beth if she couldn't pass her the note during class. Maybe she could pass a note to Alexis. She turned to her.

Alexis stared at Mrs. Robinski with enraptured eyes.

Hannah resorted to practicing crocheting under the table.

CHAPTER 15

The clouds drifted by, their cotton-ball shapes casting shadows over the yard. Hannah lay on her back on the jungle gym tower, waiting. The wind blew up between the planks of wood beneath her, cooling her arms and legs.

"Hannah!" Olivia's little voice called up from the grass below. "Do you want to play with me and Fluffy?"

"No." Hannah didn't move.

"Please, Hannah. Please, please."

"I said, no."

Zach's voice answered next. "Come on, Olivia. Grumpy Monkey never wants to play."

A muted ding-dong came from inside the house. Hannah tensed. The back door creaked, and a moment later, Beth climbed up next to her.

"How was it? Co-op, I mean. Is it fun? Are there good classes?"

Hannah sat up. "No!" she burst before she could stop herself. "They're awful. We have to take a class on *growing up*."

"You're kidding!"

"It's the most boring class, *ever*."

Beth laughed. "I was going to say I wish I could be there with you, but maybe not."

Hannah grimaced. "Maybe they would have had better classes if you were here. I'm in with the fourth and fifth graders."

"Ew."

Hannah kicked her feet over the edge of the jungle gym. "I guess Games wasn't too bad. At least there weren't any princess games."

Beth looked confused. "Princess games?"

"Never mind."

Beth sat next to her and dangled her legs over the side. "Why didn't they have Games when I was there?"

"It's just board games. But it was either that or science, so of course I picked board games. Who wants to do school on a Friday?"

"I do school on Fridays." Beth's voice was quiet.

Oh, right.

Hannah shouldn't have rubbed it in. "That stinks."

"It's not too bad. Science is actually pretty fun

now."

Hannah's heart stopped cold. *Now? It was pretty fun* now?

"We've got a really cool lab, and we get lab partners and test tubes and burners."

She kept going, but Hannah didn't hear anymore. She stared out at the yard, watching Zach and Olivia sword fight.

Maybe Beth was enjoying school. School without Hannah. *She* was supposed to be Beth's lab partner. They were mad scientists together. They were going to figure out how to make it snow on the opposing team and shine on the Packers.

"Hey." Beth wiggled her arm. "Did you hear me?"

Hannah shook herself. "No, what?"

"I was just saying that I can't come for the game on Sunday. I've got something to do for school."

Her stomach dropped like a fumble. "On a Sunday?"

Beth bit her lip. "Well, it's a thing—my mom's making me—you know how it is."

No, she didn't know.

What happened to 'it won't be that bad as long as we watch the games together'?

She sat on her hands to keep from making fists.

Hannah followed the rest of the team back into their locker room. Her first away game had been a disaster. She stopped in surprise. Beth was in the middle of the locker room practicing throwing imaginary passes. She didn't look injured.

"What's going on?" Hannah asked.

Beth spun around. She looked down almost as though guilty about something.

"We really could have used you today." Hannah tried to look into Beth's face. "I thought you were injured or something. Why didn't you come to the game?"

Beth avoided Hannah's gaze. "I just had something come up. I'll be there next time. I promise."

"Sure."

Beth had always kept her promises before, but somehow, Hannah couldn't quite believe her.

Hannah closed the front door after Beth and wandered back to the schoolroom where Mom was working on next week's lesson plans.

"Did you have a good time with Beth?" Mom asked, her eyes on the papers on her desk.

"No." Hannah sank into a chair and crossed her arms.

Mom looked up in surprise. "No?"

"Beth can't come to the game on Sunday. She has a school thing."

At least, that's what she said it was.

Mom's forehead creased. "I'm sorry, honey. I know you were looking forward to that."

Hannah slouched down. Apparently, Beth wasn't.

Mom smiled. "I know! Why don't you invite Alexis over?"

Hannah blinked. "Alexis? For a Packers game?"

"Sure. She seems nice. If you get to know her, maybe park day and co-op won't be so bad. Besides, she's had you to do something with her; you ought to invite her to something."

"But Mom." It was like asking her to let a high school player onto their pro team. Not even high school. It was like asking her to let a little league player of a completely different sport onto their Super Bowl champions team. "She *plays princess*."

Mom leaned forward and patted Hannah's knee. "One afternoon. Have Alexis over for one afternoon, just to try it out. If it doesn't work, you never have to invite her again. I'll even call her mom to invite her for you. Deal?"

Hannah dropped her hands. "Fine. But I'm watching the game, whether she does or not."

CHAPTER 16

Hannah had the TV tuned to the pregame show. She never paid much attention to it, but it felt more like game day with it on. Alexis would be here any minute. A princess coming to watch a football game.

When the doorbell rang, Hannah dragged her feet to the door and opened it as slowly as possible. Alexis stood on the porch with a backpack and a grin.

"Thanks for having me over."

"Sure."

Alexis stepped inside, her eyes wide as she took everything in. "I brought my crochet to work on during the game." She jiggled her backpack.

"Lunch is almost ready, and then the game will be on." Hannah stood there, unsure what to do.

Alexis looked around a little more. "Can I see your room?" she asked quietly.

"Sure. Follow me." Hannah took her into the hall where several doors led to the family bedrooms. She swung open her door. "This one's mine."

Alexis' eyes grew big as she took in the room. "This is nice. You have a lot of space." She set her backpack in the corner.

Hannah shrugged. Her room had always seemed small and outdated compared with Beth's. Beth had a TV and a computer in her room.

"You get all this to yourself?" Alexis had to jump to get on Hannah's tall mattress. She wiggled a little and looked around. She seemed afraid that she might break something.

Hannah remembered Alexis' small room and how she shared with Phoebe. She dropped onto her green and yellow beanbag chair opposite the bed.

"Whoa! You have a phone?" Alexis stared with wide eyes at the phone on Hannah's headboard. "Mom would let me have a phone if I didn't share with Phoebe."

"Oh, yeah." That portable phone was the closest Hannah would get to a cell phone until high school. It hadn't been cool for a long time.

Alexis picked up Hannah's book on the history of the Packers and looked at it with a wrinkled forehead.

She shrugged and set it back down.

Hannah tried to think of something to say. She should have planned something to do until the game. She was so used to Beth. They would always go no-huddle.

But Alexis didn't seem uncomfortable. Hannah shifted on the beanbag, pushing the air out like a sigh. At least lunch would be soon.

"Do you like pizza?" That's what Mom called starting a conversation with small talk. Except no conversation followed. Alexis just nodded. She looked at all of the football stuff around the room. When she saw Aaron Rodger's jersey on the wall above the bed, she reached up like she was going to touch it.

"Don't!" Hannah jumped up. Alexis jerked her hand back. She put her hands in her lap and stared down at them.

Now she'd had done it. "Sorry. It's just really special."

The look on Alexis' face would melt a ref.

"My dad got it for me," she explained.

Alexis looked up.

"*I* don't even touch it." Hannah relaxed as Alexis cracked a smile.

"I have some stuff like that in my room." Alexis smoothed the wrinkles out of her shirt. "I get pretty upset when Phoebe tries to touch it."

Hannah sat down, her tension deflating, but she was out of things to say. They sat there a few more seconds before Mom called, "Pizza!" down the hall.

Hannah took her normal seat at the dining table, next to Dad, across from Alexis. Her friends usually sat next to her, pushing Zach to the other side of the table. But that was Beth's seat.

The wonderful aroma of pizza filled the air as Mom put the pizza on the table: supreme, thin-crust. Her favorite.

She picked up her slice, eager to begin. She stopped when she saw Alexis pick the bell peppers off her pizza, one by one.

Alexis saw Hannah and glanced at Mom, her eyebrows crinkled in the middle of her forehead. "Is that okay?" she asked.

"Of course it is." Mom gave Hannah a 'be-nice' look. "Just pick off what you don't like."

Alexis' shoulders relaxed, and smiling, she picked off the last bell pepper. She turned to Olivia. "How do you like co-op? Phoebe has really enjoyed music."

Olivia's face lit up. "Music is my favorite, too!" She told Alexis all about music class and her favorite instruments. Alexis smiled and nodded, even though Phoebe had probably told her all that already.

She turned to Zach next. "Do you like your co-op classes?"

Zach shrugged, even though he had been raving about Dissection just the other day and was always trying out his lines for a play on Hannah.

Hannah always avoided her friend's siblings. Alexis was kind of weird. Oh well, at least she didn't have to think of anything to say. She started on a second slice, swinging her legs under the table.

"What about you, Alexis?" Mom asked. "Do you like your co-op classes?"

"Oh yes! They are simply splendid!"

"Which is your favorite?"

Alexis wrinkled her forehead and tilted her head. "It's hard to pick. I think maybe Crochet. My favorite subject in school is history."

"Have you been homeschooling long?" asked Dad.

Alexis sat up tall. "All my life! Mom and Dad started homeschooling when my oldest sister was in first grade."

Mom smiled. "And how many siblings do you have?"

"Three older sisters and then Phoebe."

Hannah did think of one question for Alexis. She'd show Mom and Dad right now that she and Alexis were not friend material. "What's your favorite football team?"

Alexis tilted her head. "I dunno. The Lakers?"

Hannah stopped in mid-chew and stared. Alexis

didn't seem to notice.

"I'm not too into sports."

Hannah had guessed that, but the Lakers? The Lakers play basketball.

"I like jousting, though." Alexis dabbed her mouth with a napkin. "My family went to a Renaissance Faire last year, and we got to see one! A real live joust. I wore a yellow dress." She leaned toward Hannah. "That was before violet was my princess color. My knight won."

Dad nudged Hannah under the table. She closed her mouth before the pizza fell out.

CHAPTER 17

They finished eating about when the first quarter ended. The Packers were up by a touchdown. Hannah settled onto the couch with Alexis next to her. At least now she didn't have to come up with things to say. Her focus was on the game.

"I've never seen a football game before." Alexis pulled her crochet supplies from her backpack. "This is American football, right?"

Hannah glanced over at Alexis. She ought to understand that you were supposed to give the game your whole attention.

"What other kind is there?"

Alexis pulled her legs up under her and settled into the couch. "Most other countries call soccer football. So you have to be specific."

"Oh. Yes, this is American football."

Hannah turned back to the TV.

"What's the point of the game?"

"To get the most points." Hannah opened her mouth to say you got points by getting touchdowns, but Alexis probably had no idea what a touchdown even was. She got off the couch and grabbed her football so she could demonstrate.

"Well, there are eleven players on the field for each team. One team plays offense, and the other team plays defense. The offensive team is trying to get as close to the other team's end zone as possible, so they can get the football into the end zone. That's a touchdown, and it's worth six points. To get there, they have four chances, unless they cross that line there on the screen. Then they get to start over with a first down. That line isn't really there, so the players can't see it."

Alexis stared wide-eyed. Finally, she shook her head. "I don't really understand. Just tell me which color to cheer for."

As the game progressed, Hannah forgot Alexis was there. This game was intense. There were two minutes left when Tampa Bay scored a touchdown, taking the lead.

"No!" Hannah jumped off the couch and waved her fists at the TV.

"Is that bad?"

She turned. Alexis sat on the couch, a rectangle of crochet on her lap, her eyes wide. "Did the other team score?"

"Yeah, and the game's almost over."

Alexis put a stitch marker in her crochet and tucked it into her backpack. "I'd better cheer extra hard." She grinned.

Hannah hadn't expected her to be interested in football at all. She'd thought Alexis would scoff and say football was 'beneath the dignity of a princess' or something. Alexis had no idea what was going on, but she was trying.

For her.

Hannah smiled a little and sat back down. If Alexis could show interest in what she liked, then maybe she should show interest in what Alexis liked, even if it was a silly craft. She scooted a little closer.

"Can I see your crochet?"

"Sure!" Alexis' eyes brightened, and Hannah immediately felt good about asking.

Alexis pulled out the rectangle and showed it to her. She ran her fingers over the yarn. It was bumpy in places, but all around, it was pretty smooth.

Alexis was good at crochet, like Hannah was good at football.

"How'd you get so good?" Her crochet was nothing but a lumpy mess.

Alexis shrugged. "Maybe it's inherited." She looked back at the TV and smiled. "Oh, the game's back!"

CHAPTER 18

The Packers lost. By nine points. They shouldn't have lost. They could have won.

"I'm sorry your team lost."

Hannah shrugged. "Sorry your first football game was a bust. The Packers are usually better than that."

"Maybe I can watch them again sometime." Alexis smiled and leaned toward her. "You know, if you wave a handkerchief at your knight, he's supposed to do better at a joust. Maybe we should have waved hand-kerchiefs."

The picture of them waving handkerchiefs at a bunch of football players made Hannah laugh. Alexis laughed, too.

"Oh!" Alexis pointed out the window at the wooden structure in the backyard. "What's that?"

Hannah followed her gaze. "That's our jungle gym. Dad built it when Zach was born."

"Can we play on it?" She breathed the words with awe in her voice. Her eyes shone.

"Sure."

Alexis threw open the back door and charged toward one of the jungle gym's towers. A fall breeze blew through the yard, making Hannah shiver. Alexis latched onto the bottom rung of the tower ladder.

"Quick, Princess Ruby! We must climb to the utmost peak of the castle to escape the clutches of our evil uncle, the duke, Reginald." She was halfway up the tower already.

Hannah stopped at the bottom and watched Alexis pull herself onto the tower platform. She pointed toward the house, her face shadowed from the sun. "Hurry, sister! I hear our uncle!"

Hannah grabbed the ladder and heaved herself up. At the top, Alexis danced on her tiptoes. She pointed up at the clouds.

"Look! The giant eagles are coming to our rescue! If we grab on we'll be able to fly away. Here they come!"

She went to the side with the monkey bars and put her foot on the first one like she was about to walk across them. Hannah leaped forward and grabbed her arm.

"What are you doing?"

"We have to ride the eagles' backs to safety."

If they got caught climbing on top of the monkey bars, they'd be in so much trouble.

"Why don't we grab their feet instead?" Before Alexis could protest, Hannah grabbed a bar and swung down. "They're here!" She swung across to the next bar. "Hurry, Alex—uh—Princess Violet." She heard Alexis following and sighed in relief.

Alexis landed next to her and brushed her hands on her shorts. "Good idea, sister. That was much safer." She grinned. "But we haven't a moment to lose! Our uncle will not stop until we are dead!"

Uncle Reginald chased them halfway across the world, setting as many obstacles in their path as possible. Hannah stopped in the middle of a clearing, panting. She was worn out.

"Princess Ruby, do you hear something?" Princess Violet turned a slow circle. The trees at the edge of the clearing rustled.

"I'm sure it's nothing." Hannah leaned on her knees. She wasn't sure she could handle another trap. She was almost as worn out as she was at halftime in a football game. This princess stuff was more athletic than she'd thought.

"Dragon!" Princess Violet screamed. She grabbed Hannah's arm just as a scaly, green head burst through

the trees. In one gulp, it swallowed them whole. Hannah slid down the throat and flopped into its stomach next to Alexis.

She'd never guessed being a princess could be so exciting.

"Oh, woe is me!" Alexis draped her arm over her forehead. "Has our uncle defeated us at last?"

Not a chance. *Hannah looked up the dragon's throat. Any princess as active as Violet and Ruby could get out of this.*

"We can make it!" Bracing her legs on either side of the dragon's throat, Hannah began to climb.

Alexis clasped her hands together. "Wonderful idea, sister!"

"Why does Uncle Reginald . . . want to kill us . . . so bad?" Hannah panted. Her chest had that cleaned-out, fresh feeling from breathing deep and running.

"Sh!" hissed Alexis. "We need to focus or we will never escape this dragon's throat."

She was right about that. Hannah's jelly arms slipped, and she went shooting down the throat into Alexis.

Screaming, they slipped the rest of the way down and landed in a laughing heap at the bottom of the slide. Hannah lay back in the sweet-smelling grass to catch her breath.

"Oh." Alexis moaned, stifling her laughter. "Will

we never escape from the bowels of this accursèd beast?"

Hannah propped herself on her elbows, still laughing. She hadn't had a good laugh in what seemed like forever. Alexis looked back up the slide at the freedom beyond. She looked like she might cry. She really got into this.

"Where did you learn to talk like that?" Hannah asked.

The dreamy look on Alexis' face faded as she came back to reality.

"Like what?"

Hannah squeezed the grass between her fingers. "Like *that*—'accursèd' and 'bowels.'"

"Oh."

Hannah couldn't tell whether or not Alexis was blushing because her face was so flushed, but she sounded embarrassed.

"Lydia's better at it than I am."

There was that Lydia again. "She's kind of annoying. I bet she wouldn't run from Uncle Reginald. It would be beneath her dignity."

"Princess Amber?" Alexis gasped and put a hand on her heart. "You shouldn't speak so of our sister!"

Now that they weren't moving, Hannah could feel the evening's chill. She brought her knees up and wrapped her arms around them. "She thinks she knows everything."

Alexis giggled. "She does sometimes, doesn't she?"

"Sometimes?"

Alexis laughed, and Hannah grinned. There was another thing they shared.

Alexis sat straight up. "You should come to my birthday party! Then you could get to know the princesses better!"

Hannah's stomach went queasy at the thought of a princess birthday party. "I don't want to intrude." That was what Mom would say to get out of doing something.

"Don't be silly," said Alexis. "I'm sure my mom won't mind. We haven't even sent the invitations yet."

Oh well. It never worked for Mom either.

Hannah dug her fingers into the cool grass. At least being a princess could be active. She wasn't sure how much escaping from evil uncles they'd do at a party, but being a princess with Alexis wasn't too bad.

"When is it?" she asked. If it was on a Sunday, she might already have plans with Beth to watch a game.

"In about two weeks." Alexis clasped her hands together. "It will be so much fun! It's going to be a tea party. You have to come. A princess cannot refuse her sister's request."

Resting her chin on her knees, Hannah watched Alexis. Her eyes sparkled, and her hair frizzed, just the way Beth's used to after a one-on-one game. She looked so excited that Hannah couldn't help smiling.

"Okay, Princess Violet. I'll ask my Mom."

CHAPTER 19

Beth looked up when Hannah came into her room. She lay on her bed, reading. Hannah stopped dead in surprise. Beth wore a trendy lime-green top, and her hair was all shiny. She didn't even look like Beth. It was like school was trading her for someone else.

"We have to cheer extra hard tonight." Beth climbed off the bed. "The Packers can't lose again."

"Yeah." Beth wasn't wearing her Packers jersey. They were always supposed to wear their Packers jerseys on game days.

"I know a few cheers. I could teach you!" Beth started jumping around and clapping her hands and saying things like, "Are you ready?" and "Let's go!" She looked like she was doing messy jumping jacks.

Hannah's stomach twisted. They never did cheers. "Where did you learn those?"

Beth dropped back onto her bed. "They're ridiculous, right? We had to learn them. Apparently, being on the volleyball team means we also cheer for the other school teams when they're playing. And they cheer for us."

Hannah sat next to Beth and looked at her sideways. Maybe she was just saying they were ridiculous so Hannah wouldn't know she liked doing cheers. Beth reached up to push her hair behind her ear, and when she did, the light reflected off something.

Hannah grabbed her hand. "Is that nail polish?"

Beth snatched her hand away. "Yeah, it was— uh—for the thing last Sunday. You know. We were supposed to dress up."

"Right."

Beth's cheeks turned red. "Come on. Let's see if it's time to go."

She avoided Hannah's gaze as they climbed into the Singleton's SUV. They shooed Beth's younger siblings into the back so they could have the good seats. Mrs. Singleton turned to the backseat and smiled at Hannah.

"Are you enjoying co-op, Hannah?" she asked when she knew full well that she'd taken away any possible enjoyment by putting Beth in private school.

"No." Hannah glared at Mrs. Singleton. "Is Beth enjoying school?"

Mrs. Singleton's face lit up. "She is! She's making lots of friends."

"Mom!" Beth's eyes widened. She looked at Hannah and shook her head.

Beth was enjoying school. She was enjoying school without her.

Hannah turned to stare out her window.

When the vehicle stopped at the pizza buffet, she hurried out and into the building. Beth followed on her heels. She didn't want to think about school right now. She wanted to think about football and how the Packers were going to trounce Atlanta. Maybe once they were inside, Beth would start acting normal, although it was hard to think of her as normal Beth when she was dressed the way she was.

The buffet was so noisy that understanding what was going on in a game could be difficult, but it was so much more fun than sitting at home. Little kids ran past Hannah screaming. Adults shouted to their friends as they walked through the door. Hannah grabbed a plate and started piling pizza onto it. She almost didn't hear Beth over the roar.

"Do you know anything about volleyball?"

She didn't have to keep bringing that up. Hannah put a slice of BBQ pizza on her plate and licked the tangy sauce off her fingers.

"No. I've never played."

Beth knew that.

Beth shook her head. "Me neither. I hope they don't cut me from the team."

"I thought you said you had to be on the team because there aren't enough people." Hannah reached for the last slice of Hawaiian pizza but stopped, remembering it was Beth's favorite.

Beth grabbed the slice without a thought. "Yeah, but if I'm really bad, they might."

If she was really bad and they did cut her, maybe she'd have more time for hanging out again. Maybe she'd start acting a little more like normal Beth. But Beth was a great athlete. She was good at any sport she tried. Hannah slammed a piece of dessert pizza onto her plate.

"How would you be bad? You're good at everything." She would probably even be good at slaying dragons or . . . or curtsying.

They went to the big screen room and got seats at a table with a good view.

Beth bit into the Hawaiian pizza. "What do you think the score will be? Will it be a close game or no contest?"

She seemed more like herself when she talked football, but Hannah couldn't shake the feeling that

Beth was changing.

Beth shoved the ball into Hannah's hands for their trick running play. Hannah dashed off where the field was supposed to be clear. It wasn't. Half a dozen of the other team's players were waiting for her. Hannah tried to push through, but there were too many of them. They all piled on top of her as though they knew she would be there. The ref blew the whistle.

After everyone climbed out of the tackle, Hannah sat up. The other team couldn't possibly have anticipated their trick play. She turned to Beth. Her stomach dropped. Beth had just given one of the opposing team's players a high five, as though she were happy their play had been ruined.

Hannah turned to one of her teammates. "Did you see that?" she whispered. "I think the QB might be selling secrets to the other team."

Her teammate's eyes widened. "Whoa! That's a serious charge!"

Hannah watched as Beth waved to the other team. "I know."

Hannah blinked. She couldn't have just seen that. Beth was waving at that group of girls who looked like a bunch of snooty cheerleaders. She stared.

Beth turned and put her hand down. "Just some girls from school."

She looked wistfully over at their table, like she'd

rather be with them than with her.

Hannah bit into a slice of dessert pizza, breathing angrily. Powdered sugar flew off the pizza all over the floor.

"Hey," Beth said, glancing at the powder on the floor. "Do you want to come over Saturday? We could watch a movie."

If she was making friends at school, then Hannah could make friends without her. For the first time, she was glad Alexis had invited her to the tea party.

"I can't. I've already got plans."

"You do?" Beth sounded surprised.

"Yeah." Hannah wiped her hands on a napkin and looked at Beth, daring her to complain. She'd missed last week's game. "It's a party for one of the girls at co-op."

"I didn't think there was anyone our age." Beth narrowed her eyes suspiciously.

"She's close enough." Alexis was probably turning ten, but Hannah wasn't going to tell her that. "So it'll have to be another time, okay?"

"Okay."

Hannah spent the rest of the game trying to ignore Beth and the glances she kept giving to that group of school girls. She barely noticed when the Packers lost.

What was wrong with them these days.

CHAPTER 20

Hannah stared at the yarn on her bed. She was supposed to have another row completed by Friday for Crochet. She wasn't even sure what that meant. If any of the other kids in Crochet had a clue what they were doing, she might ask one of them for help. Victor's yarn had looked as lumpy as Hannah's at the last class, and Emma's and Melissa's projects were only slightly better. Alexis was doing the best out of all of them, but even she had trouble getting started.

Alexis. Her party was this weekend, and Hannah hadn't even told Mom about it. She was still determined to go. Let Beth sit home bored imagining Hannah having lots of fun with new friends.

She reached into her backpack and pulled out Alexis' party invitation. The envelope was iridescent and said, "The Princess Ruby" on the back. Inside was a card with swirly words written in sparkly purple.

You Are Cordially Invited to
Tea and an afternoon of Festivities
to Celebrate the Birthday of Princess Violet
Please wear a dress to tea

Hannah couldn't remember the last time she'd worn a dress. The two she had in her closet were way too small. And she had no idea what to give Alexis as a present.

She took the invitation to the kitchen where Mom was stirring a pot.

"Alexis invited me to her birthday party."

Mom glanced over her shoulder. "That's great, honey. When is it?"

Hannah shifted her weight from one foot to the other. "This Saturday."

Mom nodded, still stirring.

"I'm supposed to wear a dress."

"Do you even have a dress?" Mom kept stirring.

"They're too small." Hannah realized she was crumpling the envelope and forced herself to relax.

"You could wear your dress pants."

Mom's spoon whirred against the bottom of the pot. The air smelled like curry as Mom dumped some spices in.

"Could you," Hannah hesitated, "take me shopping?"

Mom dropped the spoon and spun around. "You want to buy a dress?"

Hannah lifted the invitation in defense. "It says I'm supposed to wear one. I'll look weird if I don't."

Mom stared. Hannah scratched one leg with the other toe.

"And I have to get a present. What should I get?"

Mom shook her head, obviously in shock. "I don't know. What does Alexis like?"

Hannah poked at a crumb with her toe. "Princesses." There had to be something else. "Crocheting. Yellow. She likes jousts, remember?"

The pot started to smell burned. Mom turned back to it and resumed stirring. "We'll think of something."

Hannah looked down at the purple invitation. "And Mom? Can it be a red dress?"

CHAPTER 21

Mom stopped the van in front of Alexis' house. Hannah stared at it. She tried to pull the collar of her dress away from her neck.

"Here we are," said Mom.

She didn't move.

"Where's Phoebe?" Olivia asked from the backseat.

"She's coming," said Mom. Quietly, Mom turned, "Want me to come in with you?"

"Mom!" Hannah rolled her eyes.

"I was just asking."

She forced herself to open the door. She nearly tripped over the skirt of her dress. The dress was the simplest red dress Hannah could find, with a plain, wide skirt and just a small sash at the waist. It didn't have any sleeves, which felt weird. She tugged at the collar again and pulled the hem down.

This was so awkward.

She felt better once she had on her Green Bay backpack with Alexis' present tucked safely inside. She'd also brought her crocheting, just in case. Maybe at tea parties, princesses sit around and crochet. Hannah didn't want to be the only one who hadn't brought yarn.

Phoebe came running down the sidewalk with Alexis following. She climbed into the backseat next to Olivia, who squealed.

Alexis wore a ball gown of dark purple with big, gauzy sleeves. She looked like a damsel in distress from the medieval pictures the princesses were always oohing over.

"Happy birthday," Hannah called.

"Greetings, Princess Ruby." Alexis curtsied. "You look lovely."

Either Alexis was just really nice or Hannah hadn't done too badly at picking a princess dress.

"Thanks."

Alexis went up to the van window. "Thank you for taking Phoebe for the afternoon," she told Mom. In a whisper, she added, "She wanted to come to tea."

As the van drove off, Alexis lifted her hand and turned it from side to side without moving her arm.

"I'm practicing my princess wave," she explained. "Shall we go inside?"

The front door opened onto the small living room. Most of the princesses were sitting on the old brown couch talking quietly. Melissa held her hands together in her lap and looked nervous. She knew the girls even less than Hannah did since she'd been to only one park day. Her dress was too short to be a ball gown like the others' dresses, and she kept pulling the hem down as though she could make it grow.

"We're just waiting for Princess Emerald," Alexis whispered. In a louder voice, she said, "May I present, the Princess Ruby?"

"How do you do?" chorused the princesses.

"How do," Hannah mumbled. She shifted her weight. Her toes were beginning to pinch inside her dress shoes. She could have been watching a movie with Beth right now.

No, she wasn't going to think about Beth.

Hannah stood uncomfortably while the princesses went back to talking.

The doorbell finally rang, and Emma entered wearing a sparkling dress of deep green. She curtsied. Alexis hugged her and then announced, "May I present the Princess Emerald?"

"How do you do?" Hannah joined in this time.

Alexis smiled. "Time for tea."

She led them into the dining room. The big table had a long, shiny tablecloth on it. Each place was set with a small plate, a teacup and saucer, a small glass of water, and several forks and spoons.

"Please check the place cards so you sit at the right place," Alexis told them. She linked arms with Hannah and Melissa and took them to the head of the table. "I put you two next to me since you still don't know everyone."

She tripped as she sat down. She scooted her chair forward, but it caught on the hem of the dress. She looked across the table, but Melissa didn't seem to be having any trouble. Maybe she should have bought a shorter dress. But then, she thought of how uncomfortable Melissa looked wearing something different than everyone else. The ball gown was worth it.

Melissa smiled across at her, and she smiled back.

She finally got herself arranged. A piece of paper above her plate said, "Princess Ruby" in red gel pen, and a red napkin lay folded under the forks.

Once they were all seated, two girls Hannah recognized as high schoolers came in. One had a tray of triangle sandwiches with the crusts cut off; the other carried a teapot. They went around the table saying, "Tea, miss?" and "Sandwich, *mademoiselle*?"

On the other side of Hannah, Emma whispered, "Those are Alexis' sisters."

Hannah had always thought high schoolers were too cool for princesses, but Alexis' sisters were smiling and speaking princess like Lydia. They didn't seem to think serving tea to their little sister and all her friends was uncool at all.

Hannah glanced at the fancy dishes and sparkly napkins and the way the princesses smiled and laughed. No wonder Phoebe had wanted to come. She and Olivia would love this.

The princesses all drank their tea with their pinkies in the air. Hannah noticed she was sitting up very straight. That must be what dresses did to you.

Alexis' sisters left when everyone's teacup was filled and each plate had two sandwiches on it. As soon as they left, the party began. The girls talked about kingdom policies and the latest plots from evil uncles to overthrow them. Hannah was pretty sure some of the evil uncles were actually the girls' brothers.

Hannah tried to join in, but her princess wasn't fancy enough. She didn't know half the words the princesses used, and she didn't have any evil uncles or flying horses. She looked at Melissa, who shrugged. Her princess wasn't very good either.

All Hannah knew about was football, and these girls didn't understand football at all. She didn't have anything to say except the Packers played the Minnesota Vikings and won.

Wait a minute!

Vikings sounded princessy. If it were possible, Hannah sat up even straighter.

"Last week," she began, "my kingdom was attacked by Vikings!"

Several girls gasped, but it was in a princessy 'Oh my, you poor princess' way instead of a 'What is she talking about' way. Her idea had worked! Hannah grinned.

"What did you do, Princess Ruby?" asked Morgan, Princess Sapphire.

Hannah bit her lip. She had to say it in a way they'd understand. "Well, the QB—" No, they wouldn't understand QB. "I mean, the head knight made a really great play, and we wound up beating them twenty-one to fourteen."

The princesses all looked confused. Melissa giggled behind her black napkin. Hannah's cheeks grew hot.

Then Emma raised her glass and said, "Huzzah! Here's to Sir Que Bee!"

"Huzzah!" said the other girls, raising their glasses. Melissa grinned. Hannah felt herself smile. They'd actually played along.

Mrs. Smith came in carrying a cake shaped like a princess ball gown. When Hannah counted the candles, she found eleven.

Alexis was her age now.

She'd always seemed so much younger.

Maybe they had more in common than Hannah had imagined.

After each girl finished her cake, Alexis dabbed the crumbs from her mouth. "What shall we do now?"

Emma bounced with excitement, but she instantly looked embarrassed. She cleared her throat and said in a dignified voice. "Why don't you open your presents, Princess Violet?"

"Yes, do," said Lydia.

Hannah had wrapped her gift in floral paper with a yellow bow. She remembered Alexis liked yellow. She twisted her red napkin in her lap. Maybe Alexis wouldn't like the present.

Alexis slit carefully into the paper, being sure not to tear it. She folded it neatly and set it aside before opening the little box. She gasped.

That was a good thing. Gasping was a good thing, right?

"Oh, sisters, look!"

Alexis held up the necklace Hannah had picked out. The charm was a flower. The petals were painted purple, but the center was a bright yellow stone. Alexis' eyes shone. She threw the necklace over her head with the clasp in front. She expertly fastened it and turned it around so the flower hung at her neck.

"Oh, Princess Ruby, thank you ever so much!"

She wrapped her arms around Hannah's neck and squeezed. This hug didn't feel so weird.

Alexis passed each gift and card around the table for the princesses to admire. Once she had gathered them back at her place and neatly folded all the wrapping paper and bags, she looked up at the girls around the table.

"Thank you so much, dear sisters! I love all your gifts!" She beamed at them all. "Shall we retire to the living room for music?"

Retire is what players did when they got too old to play or had been injured too many times. "What do you mean retire?" Hannah asked. "We don't have jobs."

"It means to go to the other room," Lydia promptly answered. "Or to go to bed. It's an old word."

Morgan nodded knowingly.

Hannah's cheeks grew hot, and so did her head. She was getting tired of Lydia's know-it-all attitude. Alexis caught her eye and smiled in a way that said, 'Oh, that Lydia.'

Hannah remembered laughing with Alexis at the bottom of the slide in her backyard, and she smiled, too.

As they went into the living room, Melissa whispered, "I didn't know what it meant either."

She grabbed Hannah's arm, and they went to the

couch together.

The girls arranged themselves on the couches and chairs except for Alexis who sat at the piano and started to play. Hannah's dress didn't seem so constricting on the cozy couch, and she didn't mind sitting squished next to Melissa. Melissa had actually understood her football story at tea, and she made her not feel so lost with all the princesses.

Of course, Alexis never made her feel uncomfortable for not knowing something princessy. Hannah smiled thinking of the way Alexis' face had lit up when she opened her present. She had really liked it, and Hannah had picked it all herself, without Mom's help.

She sank into the cushions, feeling comfortable for the first time. The warm towel smell of laundry fresh from the dryer filled the air.

Alexis played several songs, then switched with Morgan, who played for a few minutes. They kept taking turns like that, some playing longer than others. Hannah closed her eyes and relaxed. The princesses were pretty good pianists.

Someone tapped her shoulder. She opened her eyes to see Alexis.

"Would you like a turn at the pianoforte, Princess Ruby?"

Hannah wriggled her pinching toes.

"I don't know how," she admitted.

Olivia took lessons, but Hannah had refused. She'd never thought in a million years she'd need to know how to play. Emma jumped up from the couch.

"It's not too hard," she said. "Come here; I'll show you." She sat at the piano bench leaving room for Hannah.

Hannah stayed right where she was.

It had to be hard. All the other girls had sounded beautiful.

Alexis grabbed her arm, pulled her to her feet, and dragged her to the piano.

All the keys looked the same.

Emma patted the bench next to her, and Hannah reluctantly sat down.

"Watch me," Emma said. Using one hand, she played one key at a time in a tune that sounded familiar. "Now, you put your hands there, and play with me."

Watching Emma's hand, Hannah tried to play the same thing. The keys were cold and smooth and did look kind of different up close. The black ones were grouped in twos and threes. They practiced several times until Hannah could do it on her own.

"Now, you play *that* while I play down here," Emma said. "One, two, three."

Using both hands, Emma began playing chords. Now Hannah recognized the tune. She was playing,

"Heart and Soul." The other girls gathered around the piano and sang along. Hannah stumbled a couple of times, but once she got the hang of it, it was kind of fun.

"Big finish!" Emma shouted. She pounded out a couple of final chords on the lower end of the keyboard. Everyone clapped and cheered.

Hannah had played the piano.

A strange glowing feeling started in her stomach and moved up to her chest. She felt warm all over. It was the same feeling she got when they gave out trophies at the end of the soccer season.

Morgan held up a camera and gestured for everyone to gather around the piano. "Smile!"

Hannah smiled so big she couldn't stop.

The princesses ran at the Vikings, screaming at the tops of their lungs. For a moment, the Vikings held their ground, but the princesses were just too fierce. They turned and fled back to their ships.

"We did it!" Princess Violet shouted. She hugged Princess Ruby. "Your idea to pretend we weren't scared worked!"

"Who was pretending?" Princess Ruby asked. "Those Vikings can't scare me." She grinned at her friend.

Princess Violet clutched her new necklace in her fist. "With my new amulet, I don't have to be scared of anything."

"Sisters!" Princess Ebony called. "I don't think it's just the Vikings we have to worry about."

The princesses all grew silent and turned to Princess Ebony. Ebony looked at each of them. "I think Uncle Reginald sent the Vikings to attack our kingdoms."

Princess Emerald gasped.

Violet held her amulet tighter. "Will Uncle Reginald never leave us in peace?"

"Don't worry." Ruby patted Violet's shoulder. "We'll get Uncle Reginald in the end. Meantime, let's celebrate our success. We beat the Vikings!"

"Huzzah!" the princesses called. "Huzzah!"

Alexis' mom came in just then. "Hannah, I think that's your mom who just pulled up."

Hannah wished she hadn't begged Mom to come early. She looked at the girls grouped around her. "I guess I have to go. Uh, my carriage is here."

"Thanks for coming!" Alexis squeezed her in a tight hug. "And thanks for the necklace."

Hannah said goodbye and hurried outside.

"How was it?" Mom asked, putting the van into gear as she buckled.

"It was okay." Hannah looked out the window and smiled.

Huzzah!

CHAPTER 22

Hannah could not get the hang of the half double crochet. She unraveled her piece again. Alexis, of course, had every stitch down like a pro. Hannah dropped her yarn into her lap with a sigh.

"Could you show me again?" she asked.

They were sitting on a low-hanging branch of one of the big oak trees in the churchyard after co-op. Alexis shifted to face Hannah. Her piece was smooth and even.

"Sure. Yarn over twice, pull up a loop, and—no, no, pull through all three loops. If you do two at a time, you get a double crochet."

That's right.

Hannah could never remember that. She couldn't concentrate today anyway. Beth was coming over for the game on Sunday like she always used to. Except they hadn't seen each other in ages. Beth was always busy with school or volleyball.

"That's my Mom calling me. Gotta go!" Alexis jumped down. "Don't worry. You'll get it. Call if you need help."

"Okay, thanks."

Hannah focused on the yarn in her hand. Yarn over twice, pull up a loop. Pull through all three loops. A half double crochet.

At the sound of running, Hannah looked up. Alexis was back.

"My family is going to a play on Sunday, but my sister has something else to do, so we have an extra ticket. Want to come?"

She had an extra ticket to a play, and she asked Hannah. Not Lydia or Emma or Morgan. Hannah wished she could say yes, but Mom and Dad always made a big deal about honoring prior commitments.

"I can't. I'm watching the Packers on Sunday with my family." She couldn't mention Beth.

Alexis blinked at her. "You're watching people pack?" Her eyes grew big. "You aren't moving, are you?"

Hannah laughed. "No, no. The Green Bay Packers. My football team, remember?"

"Oh, yes." Alexis smiled. "I hope they win this

time."

"I hope you have fun at the play." If only it was a non-Packers Sunday. Going with her would have been fun. Hannah would rather do anything than try to get through a normal afternoon with Beth.

"Maybe my sister will be busy the next time we go, too." Alexis was always cheerful. "You could come then."

Hannah smiled. "I'd like that."

"Have fun watching football. See you on Tuesday. Don't forget it's the last park day until spring!"

"I remember. See you then!"

Hannah looked back at her crochet. She wished life were as smooth as Alexis' handiwork, but right now, everything seemed as muddled as her wrinkly mess.

CHAPTER 23

The doorbell rang, but Hannah didn't get up. She stayed on her bed and pretended to read the book Alexis had lent her, just like Beth had done when Hannah had visited her. Weeks had passed since she'd last seen Beth. They'd never gone so long without seeing each other.

Instead of being excited, Hannah just felt queasy. Beth would probably be even more different than she had been last time.

The door to Hannah's room opened. "Hannah!"

At least Beth sounded excited to see her.

"Hi!"

"What's with all the red?" Beth looked at the streamers and balloons from Alexis' party. Hannah had draped them over her posters and jerseys on the walls.

"It's a co-op thing." Hannah jumped off the bed. She really didn't want to share Alexis with Beth right now. "Ready for the game?"

Beth nodded and tossed her hair over her shoulder: shiny, wavy hair. She wore lip gloss, too, and a pink shirt with numbers on it that didn't mean anything.

Football players do not wear lip gloss.

Beth pulled her lips into her mouth as though she could tell what Hannah was thinking.

"We can't let the Titans stay undefeated," Beth said, sounding less sure of herself. "The Packers had better step it up, huh?"

"Yeah, maybe we should do more cheers." Even Hannah heard how mean she sounded.

Beth wrinkled her forehead in confusion.

Hannah bit her lip. "Let's see if the game's on." She marched out of the room.

"Oh, hang on," Beth called. When Hannah turned around, she had out a shiny, black cell phone and was tapping on it with both thumbs. The phone's beeps echoed in the hallway.

Beth had a cell phone.

And she hadn't told her.

Hannah's insides went hollow like a castle after all the guests from a tournament had gone home.

Beth raised her eyes and gave a half-smile.

"Like it?" She flashed the phone. "It was a surprise from my parents. They said I need it so I can call if I have to stay late at school or something. Besides, *all* my friends have one."

Except Hannah. Because they were supposed to pick out their cell phones together, as soon as their parents said they could have them. They were going to get matching phones and call each other all the time.

Beth hadn't even called to tell her she had one.

Hannah forced her throat to open enough to say, "Cool."

Beth tapped some more. "My friends all laugh at me 'cause I'm so slow at texting, but I'm getting faster."

Hannah jerked her chin in a quick nod. She wanted to see the phone, to ask how it worked and what games there were. But Beth hadn't even told her she'd gotten a phone, as though she didn't count anymore.

If Beth didn't want to tell her about it, she wouldn't ask.

"I've got you on speed dial." Beth waved the phone at her again.

No, Beth had the house on speed dial because Hannah didn't have a cell phone. She turned and stalked to the living room.

If she had her on speed dial, she should have called.

As soon as they were settled on the couch, Beth had her cell phone out. Hannah glanced at its face. It said, "games starting r u xited?"

Beth noticed her watching and said, "My friend Liz is watching the game, too."

A lump crawled into Hannah's throat. Beth was supposed to watch the game with her.

She grabbed her backpack from next to the couch and pulled out her yarn and crochet hook. Yarn over twice, pull up a loop. Pull through all three loops. Yarn over twice, pull up a loop. Pull through all three loops.

Beth sniggered. She watched Hannah with an amused expression.

"What are you doing?"

Hannah stiffened. "Practicing. It's for Crochet. At co-op."

Beth nodded slowly, looking skeptical. Hannah squished herself into the couch cushions.

"Oh, that reminds me," Beth said. "I have the afternoon off on the last day of co-op. Mom said I could maybe come to the end-of-co-op demonstrations."

Hannah laid down her crochet. "Really?" It would be almost like old times.

The phone in Beth's hand vibrated. She looked down at it, her wavy hair hiding her face.

It wouldn't be like old times if Beth brought her phone.

"Liz wants to know if you're coming Saturday. Did I tell you about that? I'm having a party with some of my school friends. You should come. I bet you and Liz would get along great."

I bet we wouldn't.

Hannah tried to ignore the vibrating. "What's the party for?"

"For fun. It's not a sleepover or anything. All my friends have been having parties, and my mom thought it could be a good way to get to know them, you know?"

There was that phrase again—*all* Beth's friends. Except Hannah. She was something else now. Not a friend. Not a lab partner. Not a teammate.

Beth had finally invited her to something again, but with all her 'school friends.' She'd been going to school only a couple of months. She couldn't possibly have that many school friends.

Beth laughed out loud. Hannah looked at the TV to see what was so funny. It was just a boring commercial. Beth was laughing at her phone. Texting again.

The game started to pick up speed. Hannah tried to ignore Beth and to give the game her full attention. She leaned forward, sitting on the edge of the couch. She and Beth cheered as Green Bay intercepted the ball and raced down the field for an awesome touchdown. Hannah turned to give Beth a high five, but

Beth was looking down.

"did u c that?" she punched into the phone.

Hannah turned back to the TV, her arms crossed. The longer the game went on, the harder focusing was. Beth's phone vibrated and beeped all the time.

She'd given up an afternoon with Alexis for this.

Beth laughed at something Liz had texted.

Hannah couldn't take it anymore. She jumped to her feet.

"Hannah?" Beth asked. The phone in her hand vibrated. Hannah grabbed her backpack and crochet and ran to her bedroom, slamming the door. She threw herself onto the bed.

If Beth wanted to talk to Liz so bad, she should have just gone to her house to watch the game. Then Hannah could have gone to the play with Alexis.

The door creaked open, and Olivia poked her little face into the room.

"Go away!" Hannah snapped.

Olivia's face wrinkled as though she might cry. This wasn't her fault. It was Beth's.

"Wait," Hannah said as Olivia turned to go. "I'm sorry."

Olivia walked up to Hannah's bed. "Mom sent me to check on you. Are you okay?"

Hannah shook her head. Nothing was okay. "My stomach hurts. Will you tell Beth I'll see her later?"

Olivia smiled. "I'll bring you Fluffy. She'll help you feel better."

Hannah started to say she didn't need Olivia's smelly stuffed rabbit right now, but Olivia looked so happy to help. So she said, "Okay. Thanks."

Hannah reached to catch the ball, but before it even had a chance to get to her, a member of the other team jumped and snatched it right out of the air. Hannah turned to Beth in time to see her pump her fist in a small gesture of triumph.

Hannah ran toward her."You threw that interception on purpose!"

Beth looked at her. At first, Hannah thought she might deny it, but then she crossed her arms. "So what if I did?"

"You're helping the other team!"

"Of course I am!" Beth threw down her arms. "They're ten times better than you are. As soon as this season is over, I'm leaving. I'm tired of being stuck with you losers!"

"We're not losers!"

"You've lost half the games this season."

Hannah stepped closer so her face mask nearly touched Beth's. "Because you won't show up to the games, and you're selling secrets to the other teams. What happened? You're on this team, too!"

"Not anymore."

Beth threw her helmet into the stands. She ripped off

her jersey. Tossing it on the ground, she stepped right on it on her way to the locker room.

She couldn't do that. The quarterback couldn't just up and leave. That wasn't part of the game. That wasn't in the rules.

Hannah should do something. What could she do? The game was still going; the clock was ticking, but they had no quarterback. She stood in the middle of the field, staring after Beth. They couldn't win without their QB.

But it didn't matter anymore.

Without Beth as quarterback, there was no point in even playing.

CHAPTER 24

Alexis waved Hannah over to a stone picnic table away from the moms. She tried to ignore her at first. She didn't feel like being a princess today. But she didn't want to hurt Alexis' feelings. Sitting down, she pulled her jacket closed against the cold air.

The necklace Hannah had given Alexis hung around her neck, shimmering in the weak fall light. She took a paper envelope out of her backpack.

"I printed some pictures from my party! Want to see?" She took out a thin stack of photos and flipped through them. There were more than Hannah remembered. One of Alexis' sisters must have been hiding in the background with the camera. Hannah looked completely lost in some of the pictures, but in others, she actually looked like she was having fun.

"I printed one of these for each of us. Here you go." Alexis handed Hannah one of the photos. It was the one of them all grouped around the piano. Hannah was grinning just like all the other princesses. They looked so happy. She'd been unsure about Alexis' party, but as it turned out, she'd actually enjoyed it.

"Oh!" Alexis slid the photos back into their envelope. "I almost forgot to ask; how was football on Sunday?"

"I don't want to talk about it."

"Oh no! Did your team lose?"

Dad had told Hannah the score later. The Titans had scored a field goal in overtime to win the game. The Packers lost again. That had to be the first time that she hadn't watched until the end of a Packer's game.

It didn't matter anymore.

"I left at halftime," Hannah said. "It was my friend. She was supposed to watch the game with me, but she texted her school friend the whole time like I wasn't even there."

"Your friend who went to school this year?"

Hannah nodded. She hadn't wanted to talk about it or even think about it, but getting it out felt good.

"She's been more and more like that ever since she went to school. She hasn't invited me over in forever, and she's always busy when I invite her." Hannah clenched her fists, then relaxed them. She didn't even feel angry anymore, just disappointed. "We used to do stuff all the time."

A rush of giggles brought the other princesses over.

"Greetings, ladies!" called Emma. "How doth thou fare today?"

Alexis shook her head at them, hard. Then she nodded at Hannah.

Hannah pretended she hadn't noticed.

Melissa was the only one who got the message. "Hey, girls, want to play dragon?" she asked.

The princesses gasped and clasped their hands. "What's dragon?"

"It's like tag. Come on."

Melissa herded the princesses away with a concerned glance at Alexis.

Hannah sighed and looked down at her lap. "I should have known this was coming," she went on as though the princesses had never interrupted. "That's what all my other friends did when they went to school. But Beth was my *best friend*. Best friends forever."

Alexis' eyes brimmed up as though she knew just how Hannah felt, as though she felt it too. "I'm so sorry."

"We said it would be okay, that it wouldn't be

138

like all the other times, that as long as we watched the games together, we could pretend she wasn't in school. But that's not how it happened."

Alexis scooted closer and bumped Hannah's shoulder with her own. It made Hannah's throat feel all chokey inside.

Reaching into her lunch bag, Alexis took out some biscuity looking things. "Want a chocolate chip scone? I made them with the recipe we got in Ladies of Distinction."

"Sure." Hannah bit into the scone. It crumbled in her mouth. The batter was dry and salty while the sweet chocolate melted on her tongue. "It's good."

Alexis beamed. "Thanks. I can give you the recipe."

"Okay."

"Maybe you can come over sometime and we can make a batch together."

Hannah's throat closed up, but she swallowed it down.

"I'd like that."

CHAPTER 25

Hannah sat next to Alexis at Ladies of Distinction on Friday.

"We're ready for our final project now," began Mrs. Robinski.

Hannah passed a note under the table to Alexis. *Want to come over after co-op?*

Alexis grinned and nodded. She turned her attention back to Mrs. Robinski.

". . . the culmination of everything we've learned. We'll divide into teams. Each team will plan and cook a meal for the last day of co-op. You will have to stay within a budget. On the last day, we'll dress up and share our meals with each other. This project should demonstrate what you've learned about handling money, shopping, planning and cooking a meal, self-image, and etiquette."

Hannah sank back in her chair. Of all the classes to have a test in. Alexis turned to her, her eyes shining.

"This will be so much fun! Want to be on a team together?"

The entire room moved as girls shifted closer to their best friends to form teams.

"Four girls to a team," Mrs. Robinski called.

Melissa and Emma came over. "Want to be a team?" Melissa asked.

With a quick glance at Hannah for approval, Alexis said, "Sure!"

If Hannah had to do this, the best people to team with would be Emma, Melissa, and Alexis. She scooted over so they could sit down.

Mrs. Robinski passed out papers with budget sheets on them. "I've talked with your parents," she said, "and we've come up with a budget system."

She explained how much money each team had and how they had to account for everything they spent. Since this was only a one-hour class, they'd have to get together on their own to go shopping. Next Friday, they would work on decorations for their tables. The last Friday, they would have class in the church kitchen to prepare the food. After co-op that last day, they'd sit down to enjoy their meals, trying some from each team's table.

Melissa turned to the others. "We should get together after co-op to plan!"

"Come to my house," Hannah offered. "Mom already said I could have a friend over."

Alexis grinned.

"Coolio," said Melissa.

Alexis pulled the budgeting sheet toward her, scanning the columns. "Okay, let's get started. Should we spend more on food or decorations?"

CHAPTER 26

Y ou have to see Hannah's jungle gym," Alexis told
Emma and Melissa as they went into the house.
"Can we plan there?"

"Sure."

The princesses climbed to the tallest tower of the
castle. No one could overhear them there. It was time
to make plans.

"We must thwart Uncle Reginald once and for all,"
said Princess Violet.

"But how?" asked Princess Emerald.

"We will give a grand party and invite all the nobles.
Uncle Reginald will come because he is so arrogant to
think he is the best duke in all the land."

"Then," said Princess Ebony. "We will ATTACK!"

Princess Emerald gasped and placed her hand on her

heart in shock. "Not attack! Something less drastic."

"Uncle Reginald is pretty drastic," said Princess Ruby. "Attack might be our best option."

"I was thinking," Princess Violet said, "that we could cast a spell on him."

"I'm tired of spells," said Ebony. "Attack!"

"Spell!" said Emerald.

"Attack!"

"Spell!"

Hannah stared at her friends. Emma and Melissa scowled at each other.

"But we *have* to have a princess theme for our table." Emma grabbed Melissa's arm. "We have to!"

"We always do princess." Melissa looked at Hannah as though she was sure to back her up. "Why can't we do tennis or golf or some kind of sport?"

Hannah glanced from Emma to Melissa. Last week, she would have jumped at the chance for a sports theme, but she didn't even want to think about sports. On the other hand, Melissa was right: they always did princess.

Hannah turned to Alexis. "What do you think?"

Alexis tapped her fingertips on the wood of the jungle gym. Hannah could almost see what she was thinking—she didn't care much about the theme as long as everybody got along.

"We have to pick something." Melissa dropped her

hands in her lap.

"Please let's do princess." Emma looked at Hannah as though it were up to her. "It would be so beautiful!"

"Yeah, Hannah." Melissa narrowed her eyes. "What do you think we should do?"

"I . . . " Hannah didn't know what to pick.

Just then, the back door opened, and Mom called.

"Hannah, I need you to bring your dirty clothes to the laundry room."

"I'll be right back," Hannah told the princesses. "Keep working on it." She climbed down the ladder and ran inside.

When she dumped her clothes on the floor of the laundry room, Mom looked up from where she was loading the washer. "Do you need anything particular washed for tomorrow?"

"What's tomorrow?"

Mom cocked her head. "Beth's party, remember?"

Vaguely. Hannah remembered Beth saying something about a party for her school friends. How did Mom know about that? She had completely forgotten.

"I'm not going."

"Why not?" Mom sounded surprised, but she'd been there on Sunday.

"It's a party for all of Beth's school friends. I don't go to Beth's school." Hannah rocked on the balls of her feet.

Mom raised her eyebrows.

"I won't know anyone, Mom."

"You'll know Beth."

"Hardly! She's different now, in case you hadn't noticed. They'll probably spend the whole time texting each other even though they're in the same room. What am I supposed to do then? I don't have a cell phone."

Mom put her hands on her hips in her 'don't-mess-with-Mom' pose. "Don't take that tone with me. You told Beth you'd go, so you'll go."

"I didn't tell her I'd go."

"Beth said you did."

Anger flared up, filling Hannah from head to toe like the hot breath of a fire-breathing dragon. "Well, I didn't!"

Mom softened her voice, trying a different tactic. "It will mean a lot to Beth if you go."

"I don't care!" Hannah burst. "That game on Sunday meant a lot to me, and she didn't care. Having her over meant a lot to me."

Middle schoolers don't cry.

"Being her best friend meant a lot to me." The tears were squeaking out of the corners of her eyes.

Princesses don't cry.

Mom put her arm around Hannah's shoulders.

"I know things have been rough with Beth going

to school. Maybe this party is a chance to work things out."

"*She'll* have to work things out with *me* 'cause I'm not the one who abandoned her."

Mom squeezed her shoulders. "Try, honey. Just try."

Hannah pushed Mom away and ran to her room. She threw herself on her bed and buried her face in her pillow. She had to get ahold of herself. She couldn't face Alexis and the others right now. Her face was wet and sticky.

The soft knock on the door wasn't Mom's. The door creaked open, and Alexis came in.

"We need your help," she said. Hannah's back was to the door, so Alexis couldn't see her face.

"We still can't decide on a theme. Emma and I want princess, but Melissa is set on sports." She stopped as she came around to face Hannah. "What happened? Are you okay?" She jumped on the bed and put her arm around Hannah.

Hannah gently pushed her away. "I'm fine. Just—I'm fine."

Alexis knelt in front of Hannah and looked into her face.

"You can tell me," she said. She didn't add, 'A princess keeps her sister's secrets', so she must have realized this was serious.

"I hate my mom!" Hannah cried. She bit her cheek to try to hold it in, but nothing helped. "She's making me go to Beth's party tomorrow, and Beth's *awful*. She's awful. She's been completely ignoring me since school started, so why should I go to her stupid party? Why'd she even invite me?"

Stop crying, stop crying.

Alexis looked down and chewed on her lip.

"Maybe," she said quietly. "Maybe she's realized she's been mean, and she's trying to make it up to you."

Hannah looked up, her cheeks growing hot. "You're taking her side now?"

"Going to a new place and making friends *is* hard."

"Having your best friend abandon you is harder!" Words clawed out of Hannah like a dragon. "You don't know anything about it! We were best friends, *best* best friends, and she dumped me for her schoolmates. What would you know anyway?"

Alexis looked like she'd just been doused with cold water.

Hannah sat up straight on the bed, not caring that she was yelling. "I thought you were my friend!"

Alexis' eyes sparkled with tears. She climbed off the bed and hurried from the room.

"Fine!" Hannah shouted after her. "You leave me, too! Everybody leave me!"

She put the image of Alexis' face, hurt and scared,

out of her mind.

Everyone had abandoned her.

No one understood what she was going through.

CHAPTER 27

Mom would have grounded Hannah for yelling at Alexis, but that would have gotten her out of the party. Going to the party was the worst punishment, anyway.

The van pulled up to Beth's familiar house. Hannah could see Beth's window, mostly hidden by bushes. They used to play in those bushes. And they'd played hopscotch on the front porch there.

"I'll pick you up at six," Mom said.

Hannah took the hint and got out of the van.

"Try to have a good time," Mom pleaded.

Hannah grimaced and slammed the door. She went slowly up the sidewalk. That bird singing in the tree shouldn't sound so happy.

She wore a pair of jeans, dirty sneakers, and an

old T-shirt. She'd show Beth that she hadn't changed. When she knocked, Beth opened the front door. She wore a pastel green shirt and lip gloss. Her hair was all wavy again.

"Hi," Beth said. "Are you feeling better?"

"I'm fine."

"Everyone else is inside."

Beth waved Hannah through the familiar entryway toward the family room. Everything about the house was friendly and welcoming: the rickety schoolroom fan, the smell of baking mixed with a hint of cleaning liquid. The familiarity just made things worse.

A half-dozen girls all wearing cute tops and lip gloss were sprawled around the family room, chatting and laughing. One girl was braiding another's hair.

"Hey, everybody," Beth called. "This is my friend, Hannah."

Just friend. Not best friend.

All the girls waved and smiled, but Hannah could tell they were looking at her junky clothes.

Beth said all the girls' names, pointing out each one. The one braiding another's hair was Liz, the friend-stealer.

Hannah didn't smile. She sat in the armchair in the corner and pulled her knees up under her chin.

"What are we going to do first?" one girl asked.

"Let's watch a movie and do pedicures!" said Liz.

"Ooh, yes!" another girl squealed.

Hannah stared as Beth put some chick flick on the big screen TV, not one of their favorite sports movies. Beth went to the bathroom and came back with a bin full of nail polish, cotton balls, and tools that looked like they belonged in Uncle Reginald's dungeon torture chamber. While the movie played, the girls took turns soaking their feet in a tub of warm water and giving each other foot massages. The room smelled strongly of feet.

Tea parties were so much better than this.

"Hannah," said Beth in a quiet voice. "Want to do your feet?"

"Since when do football players get pedicures? Or watch girly movies?" Hannah asked. "I'll *pass.*"

Glaring at Beth, Hannah went for the bathroom. This was what Beth had abandoned her for. She shut the lid on the toilet and sat down. She'd just stay here until the party ended. She was not doing her feet.

A smell slowly worked its way into her mind.

Ugh, what is that?

Oh, Mrs. Singleton used this bathroom as the changing room. There was a trash can full of dirty, stinky diapers. The tub was full of baby toys, washcloths, and baby shampoo. And all of this was the baby's fault. Now the baby's stinky poo made everything even more miserable.

Hannah could have been planning their Ladies of Distinction project or baking scones with Alexis or escaping from Uncle Reginald.

Anything would be better than this.

Princess Ruby had been captured by Uncle Reginald and locked into his high tower. She'd been delivering invitations to the party that would be his downfall. She hoped it was just coincidence and not that he'd figured out their plan.

The scent of rot filled Ruby's nose. Who knew the last time this tower had been cleaned. There were no depths Uncle Reginald would not stoop to.

Princess Ruby had to think of a way to escape. But the field below the tower was full of harpies, waiting to encase the princess' feet in ice and rainbow-colored chains. There had to be some way past them.

Wait! What was that?

"Hannah?" It was Beth. "We're gonna eat snacks. Do you want some?"

"No."

"What are you doing in there?"

Hannah got up and swung the door wide. "What do you think I'm doing? What's a bathroom for? Now could I get some privacy?"

Beth didn't move. "What's wrong with you? You're being totally rude to my friends. They were all excited to meet you, and you're acting like a jerk."

"Me? I'm not the one who dumped my best friend for a bunch of pop-star-wannabees."

Beth clenched her fists. "I didn't ask to go to school."

Hannah felt the dragon clawing out of her again. "Could've fooled me. You've been ignoring me all year so you could hang out with those fashion dolls."

"You're being so unfair, Hannah." Big tears welled up in Beth's eyes. "You think you're the only one who's had a rough year. Do you think going to school for the first time and having to make all new friends is easy? I've been learning to do homework and go to class and every time I wanted to talk to you about it you blew me off. You're such a jerk." She was crying in earnest now, the tears rolling down her cheeks.

"Me, blow you off? What do you call texting Liz the whole time you were supposed to be watching the game with me? What was that about?"

"I was just trying to make friends."

"Well, you lost this one!" Hannah shouted. "I'm going home."

"Fine!" Beth shouted back. "You're ruining my party anyway."

Beth stormed back to the family room. Hannah heard gasps of, "What happened?" and "Are you okay?"

Hannah went straight to the kitchen. Unlike Beth,

she didn't have a cell phone to call home with. Beth's mom was pulling cookies out of the oven. Snickerdoodles. Her favorite.

"Mrs. Singleton? I need to call my mom," Hannah said. She turned away and picked up the phone.

Olivia answered. "Hello?"

"It's Hannah. I need to talk to Mom."

"She is un-a-vai-la-ble," Olivia recited. "May I take a message?"

Hannah squeezed the phone tight. "Just go get Mom!"

She heard the phone switch over, and Mom said, "Hello?"

Hannah took a deep breath to keep her voice from shaking. "I need to come home."

"Hannah?" Mom sounded confused. "Is the party over?"

"No, just please come get me." She felt Mrs. Singleton watching her. "I'll be waiting outside."

Hannah hung up. She made herself turn around and face Mrs. Singleton. "I don't feel good. My mom's coming to get me."

"All right," Mrs. Singleton said slowly. She must have heard them arguing. She couldn't possibly have not heard them arguing. "Do you need anything?"

"No," Hannah said. "I'll just wait outside."

Hannah had to pass the door to the family room

on her way out. She heard Beth say, "I don't want to talk about it, Liz. Let's just finish the movie."

Hannah slammed the front door behind her and paced across the front porch. She couldn't believe Beth, just couldn't believe her. Her sneakers scuffed the cement, making angry noises. She wanted to scream and yell and tell Beth just what she'd been through having to play with the younger girls and take boring co-op classes. Beth wouldn't care. Beth didn't care about anything anymore except lip gloss and pedicures, whatever those even were.

Hannah ran toward the van before Mom had a chance to park.

"What's wrong?" Zach asked as she climbed into the front seat. "Are you sick? Did you get food poisoning?"

"Shut up!" Hannah shouted.

"Hannah!" Mom tried to examine her face, but she kept her head down. "What happened? Are you okay?"

"I'm fine." Hannah turned and stared out the window, willing herself not to cry. Alexis said a princess has to have poise. That probably meant not crying.

This is why she hadn't wanted to go to Beth's party. She knew it would be a disaster, and it was. She knew Beth going to school would be a disaster, and it was. Everyone told her it would be okay, but it wasn't.

How can I not cry when everything is so wrong?

"Do you need anything?" Mom asked as they pulled into the garage.

"No." Hannah unbuckled and opened her door. "I just need to be alone."

CHAPTER 28

Hannah went straight to her room. She couldn't believe what had just happened. Beth was such a traitor. Football players don't 'do feet.'

She tossed her backpack on the bed. The Green Bay *G* stared up at her. Stupid, loser Green Bay Packers. Grabbing the nearest thing, her autographed football, she hurled it at the door. The bang echoed through the house.

This was all Mom's fault. If she hadn't made Hannah go to Beth's party, this wouldn't have happened.

She didn't need Beth.

Hannah spun around and caught sight of the trophies on her dresser. She'd won them with Beth.

Using both hands, she swept the trophies to the ground.

She didn't want to remember last season when they'd worked together to score the winning goal.

She grabbed the cheesehead from where it sat on the dresser—the cheesehead Beth had brought her—and tried to tear chunks out of it. She didn't ever want to see it again.

Stupid, stupid cheesehead. Stupid Beth.

Climbing on the bed, Hannah ripped the Green Bay poster from the wall. When she jumped down, she landed on it, crunching and tearing the paper. She would never, ever, *ever* watch a Green Bay Packers game again.

Photos of her and Beth stared from the corkboard where they were pinned. She ripped them down, tearing them in pieces as she yanked. She wanted to forget science, to forget soccer, to forget the Green Bay Packers forever and ever.

Just wait until she told Alexis about Beth's party.

Alexis had said, "Maybe she's realized she's been mean, and she's trying to make it up to you." She'd been completely wrong. That hadn't happened.

If Beth had wanted to make it up to her, they would have all played football in the yard and then watched their favorite football movies.

Alexis had said, "Going to a new place and making friends is hard."

So what if making new friends at school was

hard? That was no excuse for abandoning your best friend since forever.

Alexis didn't know anything about best friends.

One of the photos sliced into Hannah's finger. "Ow!" She stuck her finger in her mouth.

With renewed vengeance, she grabbed another photo but paused.

It was the photo from the princess party, the one Alexis had given her at the last park day. She'd spent all that day with her while the other princesses were playing dragon.

Hannah pulled the photo off the corkboard and stared at it. She looked happy, sitting at the piano with the others. Alexis' smile was so big, and she wore the necklace Hannah had given her. Alexis had invited her and made her feel welcome and comfortable.

Okay, so maybe Alexis knew a little about friends, but she didn't understand about Beth.

How could Beth possibly enjoy school when Hannah hadn't enjoyed anything without her?

Hannah sank to the ground, feeling deflated like an old football.

Well, she had enjoyed park day a little, running from evil uncles and wizards. It had been just as exhilarating and exhausting as throwing passes with Beth. And co-op had turned out to be not so bad. Crocheting was actually kind of interesting and mathematical. And Games with Alexis had been super fun. Even Ladies of Distinction had been bearable with the princesses to giggle with.

Beth still could have called. She had a cell phone, after all. If things were so hard for her, she should have just talked about it.

Part of a picture lay at Hannah's feet. It was one from their last experiment the year before. Beth wore safety goggles and was grinning as she held up half a crawdad they'd dissected. Hannah shoved scraps of torn photos out of the way until she found the rest of the picture, where she was holding the other half of the crawdad. She put the two halves together.

Zach was in Dissection this year. She wondered if he had dissected a crawdad yet. She hadn't even asked him how he liked Dissection, and it had been her favorite class.

She'd been too focused on herself and her own problems. She hadn't thought about anybody else.

Hannah looked up at the red streamers she'd kept from Alexis' party. She hadn't even thought about her best friend.

Beth had tried to talk to her, but she hadn't listened. Maybe at first, but then, Beth sounded like she might be enjoying school, and that wasn't right.

But Hannah had enjoyed things, too. And she'd made new friends, as surprising as it seemed.

Maybe Alexis was right. Going to a new place and making new friends was hard.

Hannah had been thinking this whole time that Beth wasn't being a good friend, but maybe it was the other way around. Maybe she was the one who hadn't been a good friend.

She hadn't been there for Beth when she needed her the most.

And when Alexis tried to tell her that, she'd yelled at her and made her cry.

Hannah rested her forehead on her knees.

She'd been mean and awful to Beth and Alexis both. She'd yelled at them and made them cry. Now neither of them would ever want to be her friend again.

She wasn't a team player or a sister-princess.

She was the scum on the dungeon wall.

CHAPTER 29

C o-op came too soon. Hannah took tiny steps into the church, going as slow as possible. Her heart pounded. She'd been so mean, maybe Emma and Melissa would hate her now, too. She clutched the 'I'm sorry' card she'd made out of construction paper, crinkling its edges. If Alexis wasn't talking to her, maybe she'd at least read the card.

Maybe Alexis wouldn't be here today, and Hannah wouldn't be able to apologize. No, she would be here. There was no reason she wouldn't be at co-op unless she'd gotten sick.

Hannah looked around the sanctuary at all the kids running around and playing. She spotted Alexis standing near the name tag table. She took a deep breath.

Quietly, Princess Ruby approached the other princesses. Uncle Reginald had kept her trapped in that tower for days before she'd had a chance to escape. She had missed all the important planning meetings the princesses had held. She hoped they would forgive her.

Most of all, she hoped Princess Violet would forgive her. Princess Ruby had been unpardonably rude to Princess Violet at their last planning meeting.

Maybe Ruby would be cast from the sisterhood of princesses!

There was no way to know but to ask. Ruby took a deep breath and tapped Princess Violet's shoulder.

When Alexis turned around, Hannah shoved the card at her.

Alexis took the card and opened it. Hannah grabbed the hem of her shirt and twisted, watching Alexis' face as she read. She wasn't smiling, but she wasn't frowning either, so that was a good sign.

Hannah couldn't take it anymore. "I'm so sorry I yelled at you and was mean and awful. Can we still be friends?"

Alexis looked up and grinned. She squealed and threw her arms around Hannah.

"Of course we're still friends!" She held Hannah at arm's length and looked her in the eyes. "Besides, we don't have time for fighting. We have to get ready for next Friday!"

Grabbing Hannah's hand, Alexis pulled her through the crowds of kids until they found Melissa and Emma. Both were looking down and not speaking to each other.

"Greetings." Alexis curtsied with her invisible skirt.

"Hi." Melissa crossed her arms. She glanced at Emma with narrowed eyes. "So do either of you have any ideas for dinner?"

Emma waved an arm up and placed her hand on her forehead in a woe-is-me pose. "We still can't decide."

Relief washed over Hannah, sweeping away a week full of worry. She grinned. This day was going so much better than she'd thought it might. "Actually, I've solved our problem."

The other girls looked at her with wide eyes. Emma's eyes shone with hope, but Melissa raised an eyebrow.

"We'll do a jousting theme! That's sports *and* princess." She turned to Alexis. "Right?"

Alexis' eyes twinkled, and she gave Hannah the biggest grin yet.

"Ex*act*ly."

"That's a wonderful idea!" Emma clasped her hands.

Melissa lowered her eyebrow and smiled. "That'll

work."

"Let's plan while we crochet," Alexis suggested when they got to class.

Hannah put down her backpack but didn't sit. Making up with Alexis and the princesses was only part of what she needed to do. The rest was going to be even trickier.

"You go ahead. I've got something I need to do."

Hannah took her yarn, hook, and the print-off of a pattern she'd found online and went to Mrs. Wells. The pattern might be too advanced.

"Mrs. Wells? I need your help on a special project."

"Sure," said Mrs. Wells as she set aside her own crocheting.

"I found a pattern, but I don't know how to do it, and I need to have it finished by next Friday."

Hannah held her breath as Mrs. Wells took the pattern and examined it.

"I think you can manage this once I get you started. It looks harder than it is."

Hannah listened as Mrs. Wells explained the pattern. It was a good thing she'd finally mastered the half double crochet because this project used that stitch more than any other. She wanted to make this the best crocheting she'd ever done. It had to be perfect.

When they got to Ladies of Distinction, Hannah

took a deep breath and went right up to Mrs. Robinski. She hoped this part of her plan would work.

"Mrs. Robinski?"

She turned around. "Yes, dear?"

"Can I invite my friend to come to the dinner next week?"

Get it all out.

"She goes to school now, but she used to be homeschooled." Hannah bit her lip.

"Of course you can invite her," Mrs. Robinski said. "Just make sure you have enough food for her, too."

Hannah smiled and another wave of relief washed over her. Her crochet project was going to work, and Beth would come to the dinner.

But there was still one big thing she needed to do.

Hannah went to the table where Emma, Melissa, and Alexis were looking over their plans. The time had come to call in the cavalry. She couldn't do this on her own.

"Princesses." They looked up at her. "I need your help." Hannah cleared her throat and spoke in her best princess. "My best friend from days gone by thinks that I despise her. I must show her that we can still be friends—" Hannah's princess ran out. "—even though she goes to school and I don't."

The girls kept staring at her, as though waiting for more. Hannah swallowed. She'd never given a speech before and didn't know how to end. She thought of a pregame pep talk, and then of a monarch addressing her subjects. She almost panicked, but Alexis smiled encouragingly. "Will you help me?" she finished.

Alexis' smile grew until her whole face beamed. "A princess always helps a sister in need."

Emma and Melissa clapped their hands and cheered. Mrs. Robinski hurried over and reminded them other classes were meeting next door. Emma settled down, but Melissa couldn't stop laughing.

"Sh!" Alexis put a hand over Melissa's mouth. "A princess doesn't get her sisters into trouble." But she was giggling herself.

Hannah tapped the papers in front of them. "Focus, princesses. We've got work to do."

Melissa wiggled in her chair until she was calm again. "My mom said she'll take us shopping after co-op today. Then you all can come over so we can work on stuff."

"Ooh." Emma fluttered her hands near her face. "Why don't you all spend the night at my house on Thursday? Then we can get ready together!"

Hannah smiled. Her plan was going to work. It had to.

"I have a plan." Ruby looked each of the princesses in the eye. "We must solicit the help of the famous Lady Que Bee."

The princesses gasped. "That is drastic," said Princess Ebony.

"It is better than a spell," said Princess Emerald.

Ruby nodded. "Only Lady Que Bee can help us to defeat Uncle Reginald once and for all. At the party, we will challenge Uncle Reginald to a jousting duel. He will not dare refuse in front of so many people. Our terms will be that if he loses, he will never again try to capture us or make our lives miserable. For our champion, we will choose the famous Lady Que Bee. If she can unseat Uncle Reginald from his horse, we will win."

Violet's eyes shone with excitement. "An excellent plan, Princess Ruby!"

CHAPTER 30

The others were surveying the contents of the shopping cart when Hannah walked up with her arms full. Melissa gave an inventory.

"We've got plates, napkins, plasticware, crepe paper, and figures for the table." She held up a bag of plastic medieval toys.

Hannah dropped a green plastic tablecloth and brown place mat into the cart. "Here's the grass and the jousting arena."

"What's that stuff?" Emma pointed to the construction paper and scrapbooking stickers in Hannah's arms.

"These are for my card for Beth. Will you all help?"

Emma squeezed her hands together, her eyes

bright. "I *love* paper craft!"

Hannah sighed in relief. With their help, she'd make the best "I'm sorry" card ever. She dumped the card supplies into the cart.

"What are we going to wear?" Emma wheeled the cart toward the cosmetic section. "We're supposed to dress up."

"Like knights?" Melissa did not sound excited.

Knight costumes would put them way over budget. "I think the theme is just for the table," Hannah said.

"Let's wear our princess dresses!" Alexis twirled as though she were wearing her dress.

At least Hannah already had a princess dress this time. Once was enough for the dress shopping experience.

Emma turned the cart down an aisle brightly lit and filled with cosmetics all in pale pink packaging. Hannah blinked at the overwhelming array of products. How did anyone know what to buy? The other girls had obviously been here before. Emma went straight to the 'Hair and Accessories' section.

"We should wear matching nail polish," Melissa said as she and Alexis moved toward a section of floor-to-ceiling bottles of color. "It will bring our outfits together."

Hannah stayed where she was, turning in place,

taking it all in. Behind her was a section labeled, 'Lips.' Row upon row of lip gloss stretched down a quarter of the aisle. She'd had no idea there were so many different kinds. Clear, blue, pink, red, shiny, sparkly, opaque. Toward the bottom, Hannah saw a package of four lip glosses. She snatched it up before she could change her mind. She had to see what was so special about lip gloss.

Emma put a can of hairspray and bobby pins into the cart. "My mom can do our hair for us!" She swung her head around as if imagining it in a fancy hairdo.

"What do you think of silver?" Alexis held up a bottle of shiny silver nail polish. "That will match all our dresses, right?"

Hannah nodded. She stepped forward, not sure why she was nervous, and slipped the lip glosses into the cart.

"A color for each."

Even tennis players wore lip gloss, so it wasn't exactly unathletic.

Maybe it wasn't so bad.

CHAPTER 31

Hannah spread the construction paper and scrapbook stickers on the floor of Melissa's bedroom. Emma knelt across from her.

"Okay, what do you want the card to look like? What should the colors be?"

Hannah stared at all the bright colors before her. She hadn't thought about what colors to use. She could use green and yellow, but that didn't seem right anymore. She wanted something different because she and Beth were different than they used to be. But that didn't mean they couldn't still be friends.

"Maybe I should use red since I'm Princess Ruby."

Melissa shook her head. "My mom says red is an angry color."

Alexis picked up a sheet of pale yellow, almost

cream. "What about this?"

That might be too close to Packers colors.

"How about this?" Hannah took a sheet of light, pastel pink. It was still sort of Princess Ruby and also matched the color of Beth's lip gloss and painted nails.

"Perfect!" Emma took the pink and the pale yellow. "We can put the cream on top for the words. Here, I'll show you."

Emma folded the pink paper in half. With deft fingers, she ripped the edge of the paper to make it look all feathery. Then she showed Hannah how to use thick, double-sided sticky tape to stick a rectangle of pale yellow on the front of the card.

"Now, do you want decoration or words on the front?"

"Both." Hannah was so glad Emma was here. She would be lost trying to do this on her own.

"Okay. Once we write the words, we can decorate around them. What do you want it to say on the front?"

"I'm sorry?"

Emma pursed her lips. "Aside from that. You should be specific."

Melissa leaned over. "You should say exactly what you're sorry for."

Hannah thought. "Saying, 'everything' doesn't count?"

The girls giggled. Alexis put her arm around Hannah's shoulders. "It would count, but it would count more if you were specific."

"Okay. How about, 'I'm sorry I wrecked your party. I'm sorry I didn't understand. Your new cell phone is cool. I'm glad you're having fun at school. I'm having fun, too.'"

Melissa nodded. "That sounds good. Why don't you have Emma write it? She can do calligraphy."

Hannah frowned. "It's not cheating to have Emma write it, is it?"

Alexis shook her head. "As long as you write the inside, it's not cheating."

Emma wrote it out in fancy black letters. She held it up. "Now, we decorate!"

"Here." Alexis found a phone sticker and stuck it next to 'Your new cell phone is cool.'

Maybe Hannah could pick out cell phones with Alexis when their parents said they could have them.

"These would go great with the part about the party." Melissa put stickers of party hats and cakes around 'I'm sorry I wrecked your party.' She'd been even newer than Hannah at the princess party, but she felt like an old friend now.

"It still needs something." Emma thought for a moment before grabbing gel pens and making swirls around the letters. The swirls were bright and enthusiastic, just like Emma.

Hannah was lucky to have so many good friends. She found a few stickers that said things like, 'Friends', 'Besties', and 'Sisters' and stuck them in all the empty spots. Satisfied, she picked up the card and examined it. It looked perfect.

She took a deep breath. Opening the card, she picked up a gel pen and wrote,

Can we still be friends?
Love,
Hannah

"She'll have to say yes." Alexis gave Hannah a one-arm hug. It didn't feel so wimpy now.

Hannah stared down at the card. "I just hope she comes."

"Princesses!" called Princess Ruby.

The other princesses gathered around. "I have sent an invitation to Lady Que Bee, the most famous knight in all the land. I have told her of our situation and our plan. If she comes to the joust, I am sure she will defeat Uncle Reginald once and for all, and we will be free!"

"Huzzah!" the princesses cheered.

Princess Ruby thought about the invitation she had sent. "I just hope it works. I hope she comes."

Violet put her arm around Ruby's shoulders. "Don't

worry. You're very persuasive. I'm sure she'll come." She smiled.

Ruby smiled, too. She was glad to have a sister-princess like Violet.

CHAPTER 32

Hannah had to make sure Beth came on Friday, and there was only one way to do that. She had to talk to Mom.

Hannah got up from her desk on the pretense of getting a drink. She needed time to think about what to say. She filled a glass at the kitchen sink and sipped it through almost closed lips to make it last longer. She watched Mom through the doorway helping Zach with his math. She wished she knew how much Mom had figured out.

Mom moved away from Zach's desk. Now was her chance. Hannah nearly dropped her glass as she set it by the sink.

"Mom!"

Mom turned as Hannah hurried back into the

schoolroom.

"Beth said she had off on Friday and that she might come to co-op."

"Okay," Mom said slowly.

"I'm afraid Beth won't come." Hannah closed her eyes for a moment and took a quick breath. "Would you please call Mrs. Singleton to make absolutely positively sure that Beth is coming?" The 'please' was important.

"Why don't you just call Beth yourself?" Mom sounded innocent, but she raised her eyebrows in a way that said, 'I thought you two weren't speaking to each other.' So, Mom knew the whole story, but she was going to make Hannah tell her. Just like a mom. *Fine*. She'd play along. She had to. Beth had to come on Friday.

Okay. Deep breath. Confession time.

"Because Beth won't come if I ask her. She hates me. But she *has* to come so I can tell her I'm sorry and that I still want to be friends. Please, Mom!"

Please, please, please.

Mom tilted her head. Hannah shifted from one foot to the other. Everything depended on Mom's cooperation.

"Are you sure Beth won't come if you call her?"

"She'll probably hang up before I have a chance to ask."

Mom considered a moment more. "You're old enough to take care of this on your own. Why don't *you* call Mrs. Singleton and explain everything?"

Hannah's mind whirled. She couldn't do that. "But—but then, I'll have to tell her how horrible I was to Beth."

"She probably already knows." Mom's eyes twinkled.

Great. Thanks, Mom. That makes it so much easier.

"Well, what if Beth answers the phone?"

Mom smiled with a little sympathy. "If you call now, Beth will still be in school. Just think of talking with Mrs. Singleton as practice for talking with Beth."

Hannah swallowed around the lump in her throat. That was it. Mom wasn't going to call. If Hannah's plan was going to work, she'd have to take care of this herself.

Hannah wiped her sweaty palms on her shirt. The phone seemed more like a dragon perched on a cliff than the old portable phone on the kitchen wall. She picked up the receiver and dialed the number she knew by heart.

Bring.

Maybe Beth had told Mrs. Singleton everything.

Bring.

Mrs. Singleton had looked sort of mad at Beth's party.

Bring.

What if Mrs. Singleton just hung up?

"Hello?"

Hannah gripped the phone. "Mrs.–" Her voice cracked. She swallowed and tried again. "Mrs. Singleton? It's Hannah."

Please don't hang up, please don't hang up.

"Beth said she has off this Friday and might come to co-op."

"That's right." She said it like a question.

She hates me! Just keep going. How would Alexis handle this?

Like a princess. Be poised.

Hannah closed her eyes and said the words in a rush before Mrs. Singleton could hang up. "Could you make sure Beth comes? I need to talk to her. And I have a surprise for her. A good one."

"Why don't you ask Beth yourself?"

Moms! Mrs. Singleton was pretending she didn't know what was going on either. Hannah glared into the schoolroom at Mom. Maybe they were in this together.

Just play along.

"We kind of–um–had a fight last time." *As if Mrs. Singleton didn't know.* "I don't think she'll talk to me."

"Well, Hannah, Beth already invited a friend to spend Friday with her."

"She could bring her friend." Hannah bit her lip. She hoped Mrs. Robinski didn't mind. She hoped they had enough food. She clutched the kitchen counter. "She has to come, Mrs. Singleton. Please. It's really, really important."

The other end was silent for a moment. Hannah rocked on the balls of her feet. Then Mrs. Singleton said, "I'll see what I can do."

"Thank you!" Hannah let go of the counter and jumped. Relief flooded through her; all her muscles relaxed. "Thank you!"

She stopped before she hung up. "And Mrs. Singleton? I'm really sorry about Beth's party."

CHAPTER 33

Hannah awoke to gentle shaking. She opened her eyes and saw Alexis leaning over her. She looked funny with her hair piled in curlers.

"Hurry!" Alexis gave her one last shake. "We must prepare for the ball!"

Hannah sat up. Her own head was tight and achy. When she reached up to pat the curlered lumps, her fingers shimmered. She held out her hands to examine her silver nails. She tilted them, letting the light fall from different angles. They didn't look too bad.

Melissa and Alexis were rolling up their sleeping bags. A yummy cooking smell filled the room. Hannah couldn't tell if her stomach was hungry or nervous. Today was the big day.

Emma came from the bathroom already dressed.

"Mom's making breakfast. Then she'll help us with our hair."

Hannah pulled her clothes from her backpack. She had picked carefully: a nice, clean pair of jeans and a new red top. Everything had to be perfect today, even the clothes she would cook in.

A call of "Breakfast!" came from the kitchen, and the girls rushed to the table. Emma's mom piled a huge stack of waffles in the middle of the table. She plopped a waffle on each plate. Hannah stared at hers. She wasn't hungry after all. Her stomach kept doing flip-flops.

Maybe Beth wouldn't forgive her. Maybe they could never be friends again. Maybe their table had the worst decorations!

At least she knew that wouldn't happen. Their table had an awesome theme. She took a bite. The waffle was crusty hot on the outside and steamy soft inside. *Just right.* Maybe she was a little hungry.

After breakfast, the other girls fought over who would get her hair done first. Hannah touched the lumps in her hair again and wondered what it would look like. She volunteered to go last.

While Emma's mom did the other girls' hair, Hannah made sure Beth's card was safely tucked between two books in her backpack. She checked to make sure she had her crochet yarn and her lip gloss. Then she checked again.

Alexis pranced out of the bathroom, her newly curled hair bouncing with every step. "Your turn," she sang to Hannah.

Hannah checked her backpack one last time and went to the bathroom. Emma's mom stood behind a chair facing the mirror.

"Have a seat, my lady." She waved at the chair. Hannah sat down and held on to the edges of the seat. Emma's mom unpinned a curler and rolled it out. She didn't pull a single hair. As soon as the curler was gone, the hair bounced back into a ringlet, and Hannah's head was less tight. She looked down. She didn't want to see it yet.

She swung her feet in little circles, trying not to think about how she'd look when it was finished. Her head became lighter as each curler was removed. The heat from the curling iron made her face tight and dry.

"Try not to squirm so much. I'm almost done."

Hannah crossed her ankles to keep from kicking.

"Now, close your eyes."

Hannah obeyed and heard the shushing of hairspray.

"All done! What do you think?"

Hannah opened her eyes and looked in the mirror. The curls hung around her face and to her shoulders. She swung her head side to side a few times. The curls bumped against her neck. She smiled.

Not bad.

"Thanks."

"You're welcome." Emma's mom checked her watch. "Oh. It's time to go. Everyone to the van!"

Hannah jumped off the chair and grabbed her backpack. They all headed out to the garage. Hannah lagged behind, enjoying the way her hair bounced with every step.

CHAPTER 34

Hannah was so full of energy it was hard to sit still during announcements. As the younger kids filed out to their classroom, Olivia caught sight of Hannah and ran up to her.

"Your hair is so pretty!"

Hannah let her touch the curls and showed her how they bounced. Olivia giggled.

"Maybe we can do your hair like this," Hannah said.

Olivia squealed, hugged her stuffed rabbit close, and hurried after her classmates.

When Zach's dissection class filed past, Zach just stared at Hannah, his eyes wide. She grinned and waved.

"What are you dissecting today?"

He looked behind him as though she might be talking to someone else. "We're finishing our crawdad."

"That was my favorite!" She winked.

At last, the crochet class was dismissed. Hannah spent the entire hour finishing her special project. Mrs. Wells helped everyone else to finish their projects, too. Alexis had been the most ambitious by crocheting a clutch purse. Emma and Melissa had both made scarves. Emma's was thick and fluffy while Melissa's was thin and sparkly. Victor had crocheted a hat.

As Hannah pulled the yarn through all three loops for a half double crochet, she smiled to herself. She finally had crocheting down. She tied off and wove in the last loose end and held the project out for inspection. The corner was a little crooked, but other than that, it was pretty good. Beth would love it. She glanced at the door, and her stomach did a little flip.

She hoped Beth would love it.

The tables in the Ladies of Distinction classroom had been spread out evenly across the room, and Mrs. Robinski had strung crepe paper from the walls. Hannah, Alexis, Emma, and Melissa gathered around their assigned table.

Melissa planted her hands on the table and leaned forward. "Who's got the supplies?"

Hannah laughed. "Calm down."

Melissa grinned.

"I do!" Emma set the grocery bags on the table.

They centered the tablecloth and place mat. Hannah and Emma arranged the figures while Alexis and Melissa draped crepe paper around the edge.

Hannah glanced around the room. Lydia and Morgan's team hadn't done princess either. Their theme looked like spring flowers. Another group had done a tea party theme, and another group had an Asian-themed table. Hannah looked back at their table and the brown place mat jousting arena with plastic lords and ladies cheering on the plastic knights. Their table might not be the best, but it was close.

Hannah didn't realize until halfway to Games that she'd been so busy decorating and admiring the other tables that she'd forgotten to be nervous about Beth. The nervousness came back, though, and she spent all of Games biting her lip and wriggling in her seat until the teacher asked if she needed to use the bathroom.

"Don't be nervous." Alexis patted her arm. "She'll love the present and the card."

Hannah half-smiled.

When Games ended, everyone else headed to the sanctuary for end-of-co-op demonstrations. The Ladies of Distinction rushed back to the kitchen to cook their meals.

Hannah could hardly focus. Beth could arrive any time, if she even came.

What would she say?

Hannah was too distracted to be trusted chopping vegetables, so the other girls put her in charge of stirring the sauce instead. She stirred, then went to look out the door into the fellowship hall. Everyone was still at the demonstrations.

"Hannah, the sauce is burning," Melissa called when she'd gone to check for the fifth time.

She went back to the pot and gave the spoon a good twist.

"She isn't here. She must not be coming."

Alexis looked up from the sink where she was draining pasta. "Maybe she's just late."

Mrs. Robinski scuttled into the kitchen and clapped for attention.

"The demonstrations are almost over. Time to get your dresses on!"

Several of the girls squealed. Hannah's stomach dropped. Maybe Beth wouldn't come. Maybe it would all be for nothing. Worse, maybe she'd come but would refuse to talk to her.

Alexis grabbed Hannah's arm and dragged her from the kitchen. They went to a bathroom off the fellowship hall to change. Hannah slipped into her dress, adjusted the collar, and made sure the skirt lay flat. She reached into her pocket and found the lip gloss. She closed her fist around it. Alexis and Emma already had their lip gloss on and were looking at each other, laughing.

Hannah looked at her reflection in the mirror. Her hair was so curly and bouncy, framing her face. The dress fit just right, spreading out like a bell around her legs. The dress and hairstyle made her look a little older, as though she really was in middle school now.

She looked different, but she still looked like herself. Even football players dress up for fancy events now and then. Dressing up was actually pretty fun. She grinned and looked even more like Hannah.

Taking a deep breath, she unscrewed the tube of lip gloss and put the brush on her lips. They became shiny and pink. She smacked them together and examined the effect. It was nice. Not overwhelming, it just added a little something. No wonder Beth liked it. Hannah smacked her lips again and turned her head so the curls bounced on her cheeks.

She kind of liked this look.

"Come on, come on!" Alexis linked arms with Hannah. "We'd better make sure the sauce is okay."

Melissa came up behind them. "I bet we have the best table."

Laughing and shouting sounded from the fellowship hall.

Emma peeked through one of the doors. "I guess demonstrations are over. Let's use a side door so no one sees us."

They sneaked back into the kitchen and waited while the rest of the girls assembled. Emma grabbed Melissa's hand and gave a soft whimper of excitement. Hannah's stomach was somewhere near the ceiling. She twisted her hands together and bounced on the balls of her feet. Alexis went to the door and peered out. Suddenly, she turned to Hannah and waved her over.

"Is that her?" She pointed out the door.

Hannah looked, and there she was.

CHAPTER 35

Beth stood out there with the moms, her face turned away. And next to her was Liz, the friend-stealer.

Hannah closed the door and leaned against it.

Just be calm, stay calm.

She took several deep breaths. Alexis took her arm and wriggled it. She smiled encouragement, and her eyes said it would be okay.

Mrs. Robinski clapped again. "Are we all assembled? Good. Remember everything you learned. It's time to show everyone what young ladies you are."

Hannah would be lucky if she just remembered how to breathe. She was having as much trouble as if a dragon were sitting on her chest. Everyone grabbed a dish and lined up at the door. She picked up the sauce and got in line behind Alexis.

Don't spill, don't spill, one foot in front of the other.

Once the sauce was safely on their table, Hannah looked around again for Beth.

She stood a few feet away, talking to Liz. She wore a skirt and a flowy pastel shirt. Her hair was wavy again, but Hannah was getting used to that. Beth was looking the other way. She hadn't seen her yet.

She could just turn and run away. If Beth did hate her forever, she'd never know.

No, she had to do this.

Reaching under the table, Hannah got Beth's card and present, which she'd wrapped in tissue paper. Her knees almost gave out. She came up right behind Beth and stopped.

She couldn't do it. She couldn't say anything. She opened her mouth, but nothing came out.

Liz saw her, and then Beth turned around. Her face was expressionless.

"Hi," Hannah finally squeaked out. She bit her lip. It tasted like raspberry.

"Hi." Beth's voice was equally weak. She fidgeted with a lock of her shiny hair and stared down at her trendy new sneakers. For the first time, Hannah realized that—even though she was dressed differently, with a new hairstyle, flowy skirt, and sparkling lip gloss—Beth still looked like Beth.

She should have seen it sooner and not felt so left out. Where should she even start?

She took a deep breath. "I'm glad you came."

"Yeah?" Beth raised her head and opened her eyes just a smidge wider. Suddenly, she burst out, "I'm really sorry. I didn't realize I was such a jerk about the game. I was afraid Liz would think I didn't like her 'cause I couldn't go to her house, and I wanted a school friend so bad."

Warmth flowed from the crown of Hannah's head all the way to her toes. "No, *I'm* sorry." She pushed the card and present into Beth's hand. "You're right. I wasn't thinking about how hard it would be to make friends at school. I was just mad that everyone had gone to school without me."

"Well, I wasn't thinking about how I was ignoring you."

"Well, I could've been nicer."

And then, Beth had her arms around Hannah, and Hannah was hugging her back, and hugging didn't seem so weird. A princess will always hug a sister. Hannah squeezed her eyes and squeezed Beth. They were still friends.

"Open your present." Hannah stepped back.

Beth read the card and laughed. She unwrapped the tissue. Inside was a little green crochet pouch with yellow yarn around the edges.

"It's for your lip gloss." Hannah couldn't tell if she liked it. "I made it in crochet class."

Beth pulled a tube of lip gloss out of her pocket and put it in the pouch. "Perfect!"

It had worked.

Hannah's plan had worked!

The room suddenly came back into focus. The smells of all the different food mixed together—Asian, English, Italian. Hannah's stomach growled.

"Come see our table!" She started to show Beth the way, but Beth stopped her. She grabbed Liz's arm and pulled her forward.

"This is my best *school* friend, Liz. Liz, this is Hannah, my best friend since for*ever*."

"Hi." Liz smiled.

Hannah swallowed.

Liz wore a pair of jeans with the kind of rips in them that come from the store and one of those funny shirts with meaningless numbers on them. But she liked the Packers, too, since she'd invited Beth to watch the game with her. Maybe she wasn't so bad.

"I'm sorry I was a jerk at Beth's party."

Liz twisted her hair. "Yeah. Um. I'm sorry, too."

Hannah looked back at their jousting table. All three of her friends watched with huge smiles on their faces. Alexis had clasped her hands over her heart.

The plan had worked.

Hannah grabbed Beth and Liz and led them to the table.

"Princesses, this is my best friend Beth and her friend, Liz."

"How do you do?" the princesses chorused. They all curtsied, still wearing welcoming smiles.

"Beth, Liz, these are my friends Melissa and Emma." They waved. "And this is *my* best school friend, Alexis."

Alexis beamed at Hannah, and her eyes sparkled. Maybe she hadn't known she was her best friend. Hannah hadn't realized it herself until just now.

Alexis came to stand in front of Beth and Liz and curtsied again.

"Do you like our table?" She danced around it, waving at the decorations. "Hannah came up with the jousting theme. It's princess and sports."

Beth fingered the crepe paper. "It's pretty cool."

Melissa grabbed a plate from the stack. "Let's eat!"

They all sat down and served each other spaghetti. Hannah seated herself between Alexis and Beth.

Ruby clenched her fists. Her plan had to work. Lady Que Bee was the best jouster ever to hold a lance and mount a horse. Que Bee mounted her chestnut mare and faced off against Uncle Reginald on his black steed.

Ruby handed Que Bee her lance. "You can do it, Lady Que Bee!"

"No need to worry, Princess Ruby." Que Bee winked before lowering her helmet. "I'm on your team."

Ruby grinned. "You have no idea how good that sounds."

"Now, I must concentrate!"

Lady Que Bee held her lance at the ready. Ruby slapped the mare's flanks and the mare rushed down the rail. Uncle Reginald came from the other end.

"Oh, I cannot watch!" Violet covered her eyes with her hands.

"Don't worry! My friend is the best jouster in all the land."

Still, Ruby held her breath. There was a tremendous crash. Reginald toppled off his horse onto the ground.

"Oh, curses!" he shouted.

The princesses cheered. Lady Que Bee turned her mare around and trotted back to where the princesses stood waiting. Emerald and Ebony pumped their fists in the air.

"Huzzah for Lady Que Bee! Huzzah for Princess Ruby! Huzzah for Princess Violet! Huzzah! Huzzah! Huzzah!"

"Hey, Hannah." Melissa poured sauce over a heaping pile of spaghetti. "Have the Vikings attacked your kingdom lately?" She winked.

Liz picked up one of the figurines and turned it over. "So what's with the princess stuff?"

"It's like a club." Hannah leaned toward her. "Kind

of exclusive."

"You could join!" Alexis bounced in her chair. "At least for tonight."

Liz and Beth glanced at each other with raised eyebrows. They looked how Hannah must have looked that first park day.

Hannah grinned. Now that she and Beth were friends again, she could have a little fun.

She clapped her hands and imitated Alexis' squeal. "You should! Being a princess is actually quite athletic. And I know what your color is!"

Beth opened her eyes wide.

"You could be Princess Pink!"

ACKNOWLEDGMENTS

I have to thank all of the people at Vermont College of Fine Arts who helped make Best Friends Playbook into the story I wanted to tell. Thanks to my second-semester workshop leader, Rita Williams-Garcia, who restored my shaken confidence in my writing and asked the very important question, "What kind of football fan is Hannah?" Thanks to Julie Larios, who forgot she was supposed to be evaluating my manuscript and read it just for fun (and who also put smiley faces in the margins). Thanks to Sharon Darrow for helping me to connect with the emotions of my characters. And thanks to Kathi Appelt for pointing out that Hannah had such a rich imagination that I should use to the fullest. And of course, thanks to my class, The Thunder Badgers. Kek kek!

Thanks to my wonderful husband for answering all of my football questions and for introducing me to the Green Bay Packers. He has always supported and encouraged my writing and takes the time to learn enough about my stories to make intelligent jokes about them, which always makes me smile.

Thanks to my family for supporting my writing since I drew my first stories on pink notebook paper. Special thanks to my siblings who helped me to use inclusive language. To my sister who read the first draft of *Best Friends Playbook* in one sitting and encouraged me all the way to publication. To my brother for helping me to hone my skill. Thanks to my parents for gifting me with the writing conference where my editor Kiri saw *Best Friends* for the first time.

And of course, thanks to Kiri for her wonderful insights to get *Best Friends* the final way to a polished manuscript I am so proud of.

AUTHOR BIO

A.W. Downer was born and raised in the Lower Rio Grande Valley of Texas. She took a crochet class in co-op when she was nine with some of the friends who inspired this story. In college, she enjoyed playing intramural football, even though her team never won a game. She spent her Sundays, during graduate school, watching football with her dad while crocheting wedding presents for some of those child-hood friends. She married a Green Bay Packers fan, and they now live in his home state of Montana with their daughter, cats, and a flock of chickens.

Photo Credit - Carl "Buz" Waitz 2018

Chicken Scratch Reading School

Best Friends Playbook
Novel Study Course

www.chickenscratchbooks.com/courses

Join us at Chicken Scratch Reading School for an online Novel Study Course for *Best Friends Playbook*. Created by certified teachers with extensive curriculum design experience, this offering is a full 6-week course of study for 5th-8th grade students. It includes reading study focus, quizzes, vocabulary work, thematic and writing device analysis, a written essay, and culmination project. The course includes a mix of online and on-paper work, highlighted by instructional videos from the author, A.W. Downer, and publisher Kiri Jorgensen.

Chicken Scratch Books creates online novel study courses for every book we publish.

Our goal is to teach our readers to appreciate strong new traditional literature.

At Chicken Scratch Books,
Traditional Literature is all we do.

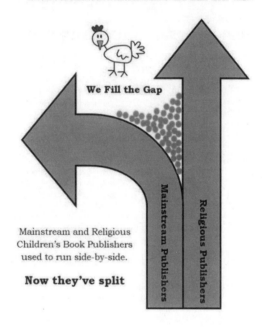

We Fill the Gap

Mainstream Publishers

Religious Publishers

Mainstream and Religious
Children's Book Publishers
used to run side-by-side.

Now they've split